THE FAMILY NEXT DOOR

THE FAMILY
NEXT DOOR

Flo Evans

Duckworth

First published in 1996 by
Gerald Duckworth & Co. Ltd.
The Old Piano Factory
48 Hoxton Square, London N1 6PB
Tel: 0171 729 5986
Fax: 0171 729 0015

A catalogue record for this book is available
from the British Library

ISBN 0 7156 2734 1

Typeset by Ray Davies
Printed in Great Britain by
Redwood Books Ltd, Trowbridge

For Elizabeth Firebrace

Chapter 1

Sometimes I wake up in the night and I think, It's still happening, and I panic inside.

It's Michaelmas again, the season of remembrance, the time of year when clocks are turned back and when the earth points out to us that living things die. Every year during Michaelmas I remember the family who lived next door.

It's rather a long story. My name is Polly Macdonnell and I'm married to a doctor who works in the hospital in Oxford. We'd been here for two years when Iain and Maggie Miles moved next door to us. They were Americans.

Perhaps you can understand how tangled circumstances become and how ridiculous it is to talk about cause and effect. Of course, when I tell you the story, you'll say right away that it was Maggie's fault. I don't agree but I grant you it's a great relief to be able to pin all the blame on one person. So much more comfortable than being rocked endlessly on the see-saw of good and evil.

It was twenty years ago, in July, they moved next door to us. My husband and I had been married for two years and already I could feel the life draining away from us. Then, like the sunlight she came. At the beginning of our acquaintance, when we were in hospital together, she told me about where she and Iain had come from – a small town in Minnesota. She said that her house was white timber surrounded by bushes with marigolds in the garden and she told me about her mother sitting on the back doorstep shelling peas. She kept describing it over and over again to me as though it were important that I should have a clear picture.

'I'm so homesick for my mother,' she said. She was only nineteen.

Our first meeting, on the day they moved in, was memorable. She was backing into her house on our common pathway, directing the dispersal of furniture, when she tripped over the ambulance men carrying me out on a stretcher. She sat on the grass, clutching her leg and emitting particularly strident American vowels. That is, if accents are detectable in screams. Then she spoke and there was no doubt.

'Of all the stupid dummko – oh, oh, I'm sorry, but aw hell oh oh oh I godda have a stretcher too.'

She had broken her ankle. As it happened, there was room for two in the ambulance.

'Polly Macdonnell,' I said, holding out a hand. 'From number seventeen. You must be our new neighbour. You'll find the hospital reasonably efficient. My husband's a doctor there so I usually get pretty prompt service. I'll see if I can get it extended to you too. Least I can do under the circumstances.'

'Huh? ... Yeah,' she said, holding my hand. I guess she was too stunned to shake it. 'My name's Maggie Miles. What's wrong with you?'

'The usual. I've just attempted suicide by slashing my wrist with a boning knife.'

She dropped my hand as though shot.

'Other wrist.'

A long silence.

'Christ,' she said. 'I wish I'd stayed in Minnesota.'

I'd better tell you as much as I can about Maggie because she is at the centre of this story. She had thick, black, wild, fuzzy hair that looked as though it could break any elastic band on earth. And with alabaster skin, isn't that how it's described? Brilliant, brilliant blue eyes with black lashes. And giggles. But what made her beautiful was her animation, the way she was never still, sparkling all the time. She talked constantly, very, very fast with a strong, machine-gun American voice. That accent annoyed a lot of people, I know, but to me it was just Maggie and I was fascinated by her Mid-West prairie twang.

My initial impression of Iain, her husband, was that he was pompous. I love the sound of that word: POMPOUS. It encapsulated his inner core, his very soul. When I first met him, he was polite and good-tempered, worked hard and had no time for trivialities. As was said about Apollonius, all his decisions were based on reason. Iain always tried to do the right thing and was as admirable a prat as one could hope to meet. Once, when he was having some expensive dental work done, he remarked that he could think of no more rewarding way to spend money than on one's teeth. I suggested debauchery and he laughed, very briefly.

But I didn't know him then and first impressions must necessarily be partial.

Iain came to visit me following my collision with his wife on the pavement. He brought her red roses and, for me, there was a bunch of pale pink carnations which was civilised of him. Three buds were broken off. He was a tall, awkward man in his early twenties with hair so blond that it was almost white. He had very large, very earnest, very brown eyes.

'Maggie told me,' he said, lowering his voice. 'If when you come home if you want to talk about it if we can help in any way we'd be glad …'

'Too kind.'

'Not at all. I think when you see people in trouble you should try to give a helping hand.'

I said, 'The world would be a better place if there were more like you.'

He looked at me uncertainly and then carried on. 'At the University of Minnesota I did a Care and Counselling Course,' he confided. 'My subject is chemistry, but I'm interested in mental health and I learned a lot of useful things on the course.'

'Such as? Do tell.'

'Well, talking helps a lot if you can really confide in somebody. Often people like you, that is of course I don't know you yet, but people who find that life is too stressful and they can't cope they're people who are perfectionists. They expect too much from themselves – does that sound like you?'

'Oh definitely,' I murmured, fascinated by this product of a Minnesota Care and Counselling Course.

'Does it?' He brightened up in astonishment. 'Then you're halfway there … uh … uh …?'

'Pauline.'

'Pauline. And I'm Iain. It's when you begin to face things

that you're afraid of you'll start to feel better. Some people are afraid to face their problem and they avoid it by drink or taking tranquillizers. I know how ridiculous that sounds, but they do – '

A bell rang in the distance.

'That's the end of visiting,' I said, firmly.

'I'll go now, but it's important to think positive thoughts. I hope you don't mind me saying it, but you'd feel a lot better if you combed your hair and put some make-up on.'

'I'm very much obliged.'

After he had gone, I wandered down the corridor to see if he had left Maggie with any positive thoughts. It seemed not. She was sobbing because she couldn't be with her mother.

I knew Maggie for sixteen years and yet I never knew her because every day she showed a different side of herself to me. She had a kaleidoscopic soul that never fitted together. The only constant things about her were her vitality and her glow. I've never been able to see beauty in those passive, Madonna-type women. It's the fire behind the face that makes me catch my breath. When I first knew her, she had three or four evening classes going and took correspondence courses in unlikely things like the geography of South America. And she talked about it to anyone who would listen – bang, bang, bang – she'd tell you about, and ask your opinion on, Flaubert and Women's Lib and predestination, all practically in one breath and in this incongruous American accent. She got us both thrown out of exercise classes for making everybody else giggle.

Then she decided she wanted to paint and she did it

seriously without the jokes. There was a soulful, bluish-purple one of a woman cuddling a child – so utterly different from Maggie herself, but when I said, 'How unlike you,' a remote look came across her face and she said, 'It is me.' That painting she gave to Simon, finally. (I'll tell you about him later.)

Maggie thought she was a genius about to hatch and she did me the honour of alerting me to her incipient emergence from the chrysalis. This is a common phenomenon in bored women. The hatching sometimes takes several years and occasionally appears to be an art form of its own.

Maggie painted most weekends. I didn't really know what was going on in her mind and so I made wild guesses. I now realise that what I thought I knew was false and fragmented, distorted by my ignorance. Look at this painting of musk mallows and see how sad she must have been.

Mag was totally different from Iain – she was dark and quick and bubbling. Everybody always looked at her first and at Iain much later. Partly it was her voice, strong and clear, cutting through our soft English murmurings.

We both got pregnant that first summer – Maggie's baby was due the end of April 1963, and mine should have been early June.

Our friendship began during the cold winter of 1963. For practical purposes we were both snowed in – our husbands managed to plough their way out each morning and there we'd be, stuck. At first, neither of us wanted to impose our company on the other one. On her side, Maggie was afraid of being thought a brash American though actually I often reflected that she was very like the stereotype that you read about. It was I who began asking her to come by for coffee because I was afraid she'd think I was cool and unfriendly, the English stereotype.

She told me how she and Iain had met – at an amateur drama club. I could certainly imagine Iain acting – by now I'd seen enough of him to guess that his self-confidence was a mask. I think Maggie started acting in order to discover who she was. She was still testing out different personalities to within an hour of her death.

Iain's parents wouldn't have Maggie as a daughter; they thought she wasn't good enough; they wouldn't speak to her. Which was a pity since admiration was the fuel which kept her purring. Then they decided to come to England which meant they were cut off from both families.

'So here you are,' I said cheerfully, 'living next door to a suicidal maniac.'

'Yes,' she agreed, equally cheerfully. 'How odd. I presume you don't want to talk about it.'

'No – '

'I mean, you seem so tranquil, so unruffled, taking things as they come, well, placid, even. So why, why did you?'

'Anger.'

'You, angry? But you're always so polite to everybody.'

'That sometimes makes the rage stronger, Maggie. But, look, there's nothing to worry about. It wasn't the first time, you know. You don't have to be afraid of me. I won't attack you with a boning knife.'

'I don't even know what a boning knife is,' she said. 'I use the same knife for everything.'

'I'll show you.'

'No thanks,' she said, quickly. Then she added, 'I gather Iain came to see you that night and did his party trick in aid of the distressed and unstable.'

I looked at her closely, then started to laugh and found I couldn't stop. 'Was he a Boy Scout?' I asked.

Her parents took it very hard – their only child going off to England. After her father died, she realised how much she must have hurt him by little details in her letters. It made it worse that he left her virtually all that he owned. He was a tourist guide who had a chain of holiday cabins – he took people to the best fishing spots in the Lake of the Woods. She said that until she was about ten years old she thought that the only important activities in life were fishing and swimming. 'As soon as we came home from school, we'd leap in the lake,' she would say. 'We were all waterlogged by October. I was a lake-child.' She said that she left school when she was sixteen and then did a typing course. She was working at one of her father's tourist offices when she met Iain at the drama club.

It didn't take us long to become friends and wander in and out of each other's minds, leaving doors open as it were. It's very exciting discovering kinship with someone like Maggie. It was our common state of pregnancy which was the strongest bond at first. Then, to our amazement, we each discovered that the other was terrified. I remember the day we admitted it: Maggie had tried to get some towels dry on the line, but it had started to snow again – I was having lunch with her that day – and we rushed out and brought them in. Then we were so cold we went into the sitting-room and squatted on the floor in front of the fire, warming our hands.

'I'm afraid,' she said.

'What of?'

'Of this.' She touched her belly.

'Me too,' I said, simply, and I felt a breeze of relief.

I rubbed my knees rhythmically as Maggie went on, 'I'm such a coward. I blubber when I've got a toothache. Afterwards, nobody's going to say how wonderful I was because I fully expect to be an hysterical half-wit. I know I will.' Her eyes were tearful.

'It's silly because everybody goes through it,' I said at last, 'at least, most women.'

'I mean – if – if things have to go on, it doesn't matter if here and there a woman dies, but it does matter to us in case we're her.'

'Like being struck by lightning – monumentally important when it happens to you,' I said, and then, after a moment, 'Do you think "fortitude" is simply a euphemism for dumb terror?'

'I know at the very first pain I'm going to start shrieking and telling the nurse that I've changed my mind … I don't want the baby … take it away … back to the drawing-board … start again … do not pass Go … let's do a U-turn … quick, into reverse … turn back … I've had second thoughts … back-pedal … I'm a cowardly jellyfish … I've got cold feet … let's not do anything hasty … I'll lead a good life from now on … I'll join a nunnery.'

'Too late now to go back to the Garden of Eden, Mag. We've eaten the apple.

"Adam lay a-shackled, a-shackled in his chains,
A thousand years a-shackled, a-shackled Adam lay,
And all was for an apple, an apple that he ate,
And all was for an apple, dear, on a summer day." '

'All that for one lousy apple? It was probably one of those tasteless Golden Delicious too. I can't imagine a Granny Smith doing it ... Oh, I'm too young to die,' she said, and we both laughed for too long because, you see, we really were afraid. Just then the doorbell rang.

'It's probably the door-to-door brush salesman. I saw one across the road yesterday.'

'Maybe it's the Angel of Death come to tell us our time is up?'

'I'll answer it, if you like,' I said. 'If it's the brush salesman, do you want anything?'

She yawned. 'Just say, "Not today, thank you." '

I came back giggling.

'It was a chap saying, "Are you interested in the salvation of your soul, your eternal soul?" They were Mormons, impeccably dressed.' I had suddenly realised that with their Mid-West American accents they reminded me of ... oh God ... of Iain.

'So what did you say?'

'I said what you told me to. I said, "Not today, thank you." '

We both sat on the floor, rocking with laughter.

I've thought of Maggie and Iain so much over these past few years and it's my opinion that they married too young.

16

They were just children, jelly-like and amorphous. They were propelled by physical passion, without thought. I suppose most people marry under those circumstances and I suppose in the long run it's all right. Like childbirth. But the pain and the shock in individual cases when individual couples discover what an appalling mistake they've made – one wishes one could warn them, but you know that's not possible. You feel you want to throw yourself across the bride's path as she proceeds so single-mindedly down that fearful aisle. They, both of them, simply married the first person they were physically attracted to, knowing nothing beyond those few square miles in rural Minnesota. You might say that the early marriage gave them time to work at things and improve them, but I don't think it happens like that very often. Then when she got pregnant the marital knot was tied as tight as it could go. You're pinned when a child is due.

Oh bitter, bitter woman, I hear you say. Eaten the proverbial sour grapes and her teeth are set on edge. Let me just tell her (you're getting into your stride now) how sorry I feel for her husband having to put up with this neurotic virago who's costing the National Health Service a fortune with her faked suicide attempts (and her husband a doctor too – how embarrassing for him, poor chap!). Small wonder if one of these fine days he just ignores her and lets her die. Serve her jolly well right, that's what I say.

Dear Reader, thank you for taking the time and trouble to analyse my character. These thoughts have, oddly enough, occurred to me from time to time too. Be assured that I will keep them in mind. (Next time don't call me, I'll call you.)

17

I don't know how Maggie's and Iain's marriage went. You don't know things like that from the outside. But, of course, these walls are thin. You can hear any fights which occur.

Oh, but Maggie was beautiful with that black hair and those brilliant blue eyes and those very small white teeth and everything about her shimmering. The whole of her – she was so human and vulnerable. She put meaning into my existence. It's not what you're thinking. I did love her, but not that way, you know. I started by feeling sorry for her because she was so far from home and especially having her first baby. She said the doctors and nurses were different from the ones in America and she didn't like it. The health visitors all made her cry because they were so bossy. Iain was good to Maggie at that time, very gentlemanly and protective.

On 3rd May 1963, Mag had a girl – Isabella Berenice – but because she developed a sneeze in her second week, everybody called her Tishy. She was eight pounds exactly.

I remember the day well. The tulips were just starting to come up because of the bad weather. Iain poked his head in to say that Mag had started, and I stood at my window and watched them drive off towards the hospital; I felt that I'd been left on one side of a chasm and that I had to step over it before I could join Maggie again. I turned to John for comfort. I guess I haven't mentioned him before. He's my husband. He doesn't come into the story much.

I know this is going to be a problem for some of you readers; you're wondering how I can tell a story spanning twenty years of married life and not consider my husband an important part of it. Yes, it is odd, but all I can say is that that was the way it was: he wasn't important to me. If it makes you feel more comfortable, I'll try to bring him into the story from time to time when I think of it. His personality? You want me to tell you what sort of a man he was in those days? Kind, good, hard-working, patient, very tired, decent. You say that 'doesn't bring him alive'? No, I guess it doesn't.

I visited Maggie the next day and found that she was not happy.

'When I say perhaps I'm doing something wrong, I do wish all these midwives or whatever you call them wouldn't agree with such alacrity. It seems to give them a surge of joy when they see an American struggling. They imply that motherhood comes naturally to all English-women.'

But for me, it was all for nothing ...

My son was born three days later and I named him Timothy Daniel. He was hydrocephalic and his inner organs – liver and kidneys – they weren't normal either. He lived three weeks. Before I left hospital, I had my Fallopian tubes tied – the doctors said it wasn't safe for me to be pregnant again. There, I've told you and I don't think I want to talk about it any more.

I was in hospital for five weeks – it isn't easy to give birth to a hydrocephalic child. After I came home, I went over to Maggie's and she was terribly embarrassed to see me. She stammered and shuffled and looked at the floor.

'How are you?'

'Overjoyed by the wonder and mystery of life,' I said.

'I've been thinking about you. I hope you're not going to …'

'No, I'm not going to … as you put it. As Iain has helpfully said, I must accept what cannot be changed and count my blessings. The hospital gave me a splendid cassette on transcendental meditation which should make me wise and good. Or something.'

'You can try again.'

'Indeed, I can try till I'm blue in the face. Lot of good it'll do me. I've had my tubes tied. How's your little bundle of joy?'

'Oh Polly, I'm sorry.'

'Whatever for?'

'I'm sorry, I keep saying the wrong thing. Maybe we should start again. Hello, Polly.'

'Look, Maggie,' I said, 'I'm raw and sore now, but then I've gone through most of my life feeling that I've just been skinned alive. It's not a new experience. I can either shower you with talk of Blackness and Despair which (a) isn't strictly accurate and (b) you wouldn't understand anyhow or else I can be flippant. So don't stand there writhing and apologising. I'm in a cesspool of my own making or, if you like, I've made my bed and I must lie on it.'

But as time passed, I began to tell her about Timothy. Just by talking about him he took shape and substance again in my mind. He had been an ugly little brute, being vigorously hydrocephalic, but he was my baby. Oh, boo hoo.

I put my head on her shoulder and she said, 'Tell me about it, please,' and so I told her all about him, how it had been a terrible birth, but I hadn't known there was anything wrong, and the nurse saying, 'It's all right now, it's all right now, it's all right now,' over and over again and bathing my forehead – and me saying, 'Is it a boy?' and how the nurse said, 'Yes,' and me saying 'Is he all right?' and the nurse saying 'Well, you know, my dear, it was a difficult birth,' and me then saying, 'Is he not all right then?' and how the nurse said, 'No, he isn't,' and how I drifted off to sleep, worried, and the doctors asking me the next day had I had German measles or any other diseases early on or had I been on the Pill or taken any drugs during pregnancy and me saying no, no, and them checking when I 'last tried to hurt myself ' as they put it and me saying before I got pregnant and finally asking, well, what exactly is wrong with him and how they said, he's hydrocephalic and how I held him one afternoon in my arms for over an hour and how dreadful he looked and how I would have given my life for my son and how I crept down to the bottom of the bed when the curtains were drawn for the bedpan and took all my medical notes and read them and found out all about the terrible damage to his kidneys and liver and them suggesting I should be given a Wasserman in case it was all due to congenital syphilis and how I carefully put the notes back the next time the curtains were drawn around me for the bedpan and how later that day the doctor casually said he'd like to give me a blood test and how I said I haven't got VD and him saying *of course* you haven't, whatever gave you *that* idea and how the next time I looked my notes had been removed from the end of the bed and how later I asked the nurse what was the result of the Wasserman and she said, how did you know it was a Wasserman? and I said, just because I'm in bed, I'm not

21

stupid and she said it was negative, we don't know why your baby was born that way and you're not supposed to read your notes, you know, and I said why the hell not? and three weeks later they said, he died this morning, it's all for the best, and how empty I felt, that the pregnancy was truly over and how I began talking to myself and how they gave me a pile of hospital linen to mend to keep my mind from morbid thoughts they said and how I said to John if you don't get me out of this bloody hole I shall go mad and how I came home the next morning. I told Maggie everything.

'How did you know that I wanted to talk about him?' I asked her much later. 'Weren't you afraid I'd be upset? I might have gone all chilly and told you not to rush in where angels fear to tread, all that sort of thing.'

'I don't know,' she admitted, puzzled.

'John said it was better that he should die, all things considered.'

'Men,' she muttered. She looked defiant for a moment. 'I've got something to tell you too. It's hard to say it because you might punch me in the face, but I feel I've been run over by a steam roller. Squashed. Obliterated. Forced to keep walking about squirting milk while somebody shines bright lights in my eyes. I didn't really want this baby.'

'Aw, Maggie. Oh. You bitch.'

'Yeah, I know. What are you going to do about it?'

We both looked away, because we couldn't say anything.

'It's a helluva life, isn't it?' she finally said. 'Whatever you do, you get slapped across the face by a slimy fish.'

'Yes.'

She walked back and forth restlessly. Her hands were raw

and her hair was greasy and tied back tightly into a knot. She actually looked ugly.

'Oh, I'm saying the wrong things,' she stammered.

'It's straightforward,' I said. 'You've got a living baby and I've got a dead one.'

'Don't – '

'No.'

'Shit, shit, shit, what can anyone say?'

'I think you've found the *mot juste*, inelegant though it may be. Let's start again. I'm all right. How are you?'

'Fine, thank you,' she said bleakly. There was a silence.

Maggie's baby was lying in a carry-cot on a shiny red chair beside a parchment lamp which had a Chianti bottle for its base and near some striped red and cream curtains. For years afterwards Tishy Miles was fixed in my mind – no, not 'for years', but forever – Tishy is fixed forever in all her vulnerability in that red chair by those red curtains and the Chianti bottle and it's something that makes me want to cry because I'm brought around to thinking how we all had our beginnings in helplessness and I feel a cramp in my heart connected with it that I can't quite understand – something about the brevity and fragility of human life.

'She's a beautiful little bugger,' I said. 'Lucky you.' She was a brown-eyed blonde with universal baby features.

'Yes. Truly, I'm sorry about ...' she began.

'You look ill,' I said, and she flinched. From where I was sitting, I could see her wedding photograph, her and Iain, and I noticed again how young and painfully untried they looked in the picture. She saw me looking and smiled.

23

'Don't we look gawky?' she said. 'Were you like that too, on your wedding day?'

'I was a bit fuzzled. I got cold feet when it was time to set out for the church, said I wasn't going to do it and somebody poured a tumbler of whisky down my throat. Can't remember most of the rest of the day … Look here, she's lovely – you know, as babies go.'

We laughed and felt at ease.

'Who do you think she looks like?' Maggie asked.

'Well, she's got Iain's eyes and hair.' But pray God she doesn't inherit his sparkling personality, I thought.

'I feel awful,' Maggie said.

'Yes, I know. Why?'

'I know that it's a cliché to say a great cloud has come down over me but I don't know any other way of saying it. It came down over me about two days after, and it's getting worse.' She began to snuffle.

'You're speaking to the expert on clouds.'

'Oh, heavens, I don't mean like *that*. It's not *that* bad.'

'Actually, it clears the decks marvellously.'

She got over the depression without trying my solution of course. I watched Tishy grow up. When she was little, Iain and Maggie fought all the time. That myth about two people being made into one … well.

I leaned over the back fence one day and asked Iain, who was in a deckchair, what he was reading. He stood up and closed the book, keeping his finger in place as a marker.

'You'd laugh,' he said. 'It's about stress management.'

I said nothing.

'The point is, you're supposed to talk to someone you

really trust when things get bad. But when things get bad, you don't trust anybody. Maybe that's *why* things get bad.'

'Maybe.'

'Trouble is … advice is useless.'

'The beginning of wisdom,' I said.

In her earliest years, Tishy was a happy child, serene, quite unlike Maggie with her nervous brilliance. Tish, in fact, was like Iain with his conventional view of the world. Though Iain, as time went on, became much more bitter and cynical. It's something that often happens to quiet people who spend a lot of their time trying to figure out their place in the system. They notice things which slip past the scintillating ones.

I didn't pretend to know Tish as well as I knew Maggie, so perhaps what little I did know was more accurate. When you know someone is a mystery, you keep your eyes open, you're always observing, always ready to learn and add to your knowledge and so you're more aware of changes and what they're doing than you are with somebody you think you know. You could see Tish grow and change from day to day. She always felt herself a failure. Iain and Maggie saw to that, well and truly.

It's difficult to explain to parents that their child just *is* and that they should be profoundly grateful, but self-interest and selflessness are so mingled that it's impossible to unravel them. They see the child as their second chance, and I suppose it's not surprising.

In all their arguments, they seemed to settle it that Iain was the boss. Well, settled in a very impermanent way. Iain relished it rather more than was comfortable.

She said dreadful, cruel things about him behind his back. I suppose she felt bitter and she tried to rebel in small ways. Somehow they seemed to arrive at their decisions in the wrong way. Perhaps it was just that they never had any serious problems to face together, or at least not until it was too late.

I went back to teaching at our local primary school the year after Timothy and then, five years later, Maggie decided that being a housewife with Tish at school all day wasn't enough, and she got herself into our local college of education to train as a teacher. God knows how she got in – or through. Charm, I suppose. She couldn't add and she couldn't spell. She was lucky that we were just on the edge of that shortage of teachers and they were still taking most applicants. Derek Lloyd, my headmaster, hired her because she was a friend of mine – and because he liked her looks. It turned out to be a mistake.

I suppose Maggie and Iain believed they were doing the right thing, trying to make the best of a bad job. Perhaps Iain thought of it as a Challenge to Accept what Cannot be Changed.

Sometimes I would get cross with Maggie. 'You're a strong and healthy woman. Stop wasting pity on yourself and think of someone who really needs compassion.'

'You?' she said.

'No, of course not me,' I snapped. 'I'm just thinking that all you need to do is sneeze and you'll have half a dozen friends patting your arm. So why complain?'

'I don't want half a dozen friends telling me how much they care. I want one man who *shows* me.'

26

'Ho hum.'

Back to Tishy: Iain and Maggie repeated all the proper things about respecting her autonomy and granting that she had a right to choose her own interests, that they couldn't force her, loving her for her own sake, all that sort of thing. And they were terribly, terribly disappointed.

I remember Tish trying to tell me in one of her occasional moments of articulation.

'Daddy says I shouldn't watch television because he didn't have it when he was a little boy. He says I'm like a slug.'

'What does he think you should be doing?'

'Hobbies,' she said, glumly. She brooded. 'I worry,' she said, finally. 'I think there's something wrong with my Mum.'

'What?'

Her eyes went wet and she began crying, very convulsively.

'Tell me,' I said a little crossly. 'What are you talking about?'

'I can't tell you.' Clearly, she had inherited Maggie's taste for melodrama. 'Nobody likes me. They laugh at me. Catherine Davies is always saying I'm stupid and laughing at me. When we go up to ask the teacher something, she laughs at what I say and calls me Stupid.'

'Don't be silly,' I said uneasily. 'Just call her Stupid back again.' I thought at once that that was a foolish remark but it was difficult to know what to say instead. Just ignore her? That was pretty useless advice too.

She looked at me with her deep, deep brown eyes.

27

'I do call her Stupid. But then she says I'm empty between the eyes and thick as two short planks and stuff like that and I can't keep up with her.'

'Effective abuse is an art,' I admitted. 'I could give you about seventy-five words for "stupid", all of which I've used on myself from time to time, but I don't think it would be much help.'

'No. They say I stink. I tell them they stink right back again. That's what my Mum told me to say.'

'But you don't stink, Tish,' I said, laughing, but genuinely puzzled.

'I think I do,' she said in a low voice. 'Anyhow you don't understand. It's not important. Mrs Hallson doesn't like me. "Isabella Miles" she says – and she doesn't pay any attention to me.'

'She's probably got her hands full dealing with the others while you get on with your work,' I said with a twinge of recognition. 'Anyhow, doesn't she call you Tishy?'

'No, it's always Isabella. Stupid name. And I always get into trouble and I don't like it. She picks on me, she always thinks it's me and it isn't. She nags and nags at me to keep working. So does Dad.'

'I can imagine,' I said with a sigh. Iain believed in Giving of One's Best. All the time. Then I added, 'Do you work?'

'I try. I try hard. But my writing isn't very good. I try. But nobody cares about what I do. I know they don't. I keep trying. It's just the handwriting. It isn't my fault. I try. Mum and Dad get so angry and then they say they'll give me a treat if I do better and I try so hard, but it's never good enough and I never get anything. I pray every night and I

28

promise the next day I'll try even harder but they're never pleased with me. Dad says he did much better when he was my age and he shows me his reports from school and I can't do that well no matter how hard I try. It's not fair. I hate everybody, just everybody.'

Then she went home and I brooded over what she had said and what she was going through.

Meanwhile, over the years. Maggie and I had formed a solid bond of friendship. We were both buckled and unbalanced, each in our own unique way, but we managed to converge awkwardly like pieces in an ill-made puzzle.

I'd better tell you about the set-up at the school. We were in an outside Nissan hut built during the war to take the influx of children from London – meant to be temporary but it just stayed. The hut was divided into two classrooms by a partition – I had one and Maggie had the other. We had to rely upon one another all the time since we were cut off from the main building. That's how our friendship was finally cemented. We'd lived next door to the Mileses for years and had been in and out of each other's houses and lots of fun and chatter, but working together – that's different – talking first thing in the morning before the children arrived, hearing each other shout (the walls are so thin), breaking down and telling the other one what a vile day we'd had, sharing worries, admiring each other's classroom walls and decorations – that sort of thing. If you like each other to start with, then before you know it you've formed a real bond. And I did like her so much even though she was wildly disorganised. She was the most spontaneously open person I'd ever met. She made me laugh and I felt protective and maternal towards her partly because I was seven years older than she was. It happened long enough ago, you'd have thought I'd have got over it by now.

She was marvellously kind. I remember when one particularly ghastly child announced that he was going to be sick, opened up his locker desk and, with a great whoop, proceeded to vomit all over his books and equipment. There I was, ten minutes later, gagging and retching and poking around in the warm seething mass with a ruler, wondering what I could salvage when Maggie came in from the other room.

'Oh, does that bother you?' she asked. 'Things like that don't upset me at all. You go and take my class and I'll clean it up.'

'Oh – I couldn't,' I said, seizing up every time a wave of sick drifted up to me.

'Look, I'm supposed to be teaching them fractions and I'm getting all in a muddle. You straighten them out and I'll deal with this.'

'Are you *quite* sure?'

'Absolutely. Now do be a dear and go and tell them about lowest common denominators, whatever they are.'

So I did and when I came back twenty minutes later the room was sweet and clean and smelling of Dettol with no sign whatever of Peter Tanning's gastric crisis. A thing like that binds you to a person for life.

'Perhaps you should learn how to do simple arithmetic before you set about teaching it,' I suggested soon after this.

Her reaction to this unremarkable proposition was astonishment.

'But why? I've got you in the next room. Isn't that what team teaching is all about?'

'Not exactly, Maggie.'

She was more fun to be with than anyone else I have ever known. You can see by this picture what glorious hair she had – it had reddish-brown bits of glow in it to liven up the darkness. Look how wild it was – all in a frizz of fire and vitality. You can see her features were straight and delicate and gentle. Not that gentleness was a quality that you noticed about her. She had far too much exuberance for that. I didn't exactly love her, but each day when I got up, I thought with pleasure, I'm going to see Maggie today. No, not sexual, but physical because she was so funny and so lively. She brought life into the boring old classroom. There are huge areas of human affection for which there isn't an exact word. 'Friendship' is the closest but there was more to it than that.

I found it very difficult to get to know Iain for a long time, even living next door to him. But as time passed, I found that he was not nearly as shallow and predictable as I had at first thought. In fact, he was a deeper, more complex person than Maggie – now she was pretty transparent. But Iain was quieter and perhaps more bitter. His Positive Outlook on Life was actually quite a thin veneer. He observed randomly while she was more selective about the things she decided to notice.

I fell into step with him one Sunday afternoon as we both set out to post letters.

'How are you these days, I mean – really?'

His voice was so gentle and subdued that I hesitated to

chirp, 'Fine, thank you. And you?' which is my usual response to polite enquiries. For a moment, I didn't know how to answer.

'Fine, thank you. And you?'

'No, you're not. I saw the ambulance on Friday night. I know I can't help. I was stupid – before – and I know I'll be stupid again – there are sometimes just rays of light when – when a person realises how stupid they've been – and will probably keep on being, if I'm making sense.'

'Yes, you're making sense. Go on.'

'There's nothing else to say except I want you to know I'm sorry.'

We trudged back from the post box in silence.

'Iain.'

'Yes?'

'Thank you very much. I didn't give you enough credit for ...'

'Having any sense?' He laughed uncomfortably. 'I don't, actually. It's that I'm depressed today. By tomorrow, I'll be telling you to grasp the nettle with both hands and face your fears.'

I laughed too. 'I'm sorry you're depressed. I could suggest that you look on the bright side, but that would be mean.'

'No, it wouldn't. It's very helpful advice. It's just that ...'

'I know,' I said.

But I was talking about the two of them. They made a superb couple while they were showing off together. He had intended to get a university post eventually but he was so worried when Maggie's pregnancy was confirmed that he gratefully stuck with his job at the poly. His subject was chemistry. In the beginning, Maggie was bowled over that such an intelligent man should treat her as though she were an intelligent woman. Not that it was her intellect that he was responding to, I imagine. But he gradually grew into a bully because of a sense of failure. She'd married him because she thought he was superior to her and he had to maintain the image at all costs.

And Tish – when she was little, she was extremely delicate, fine-boned, fragile. She had Iain's fair colouring – long, white-gold hair and his deep brown eyes – but she had Maggie's features. She had the potential for beauty, but only the potential – she never really flowered. She looked a bit as though she'd been sat upon at an early stage.

Tishy and I got on well. I learned from the beginning not to take liberties. She couldn't bear to be touched which was odd. I'm the sort of teacher who flings my arms around the children all the time. I do it without thinking and the first time I did it to Tish, I felt her go rigid. Of course I stopped right away and said, 'What's wrong?'

'Nothing,' she said, still stiff. I took my arm away. But I kept forgetting and each time I felt her freeze. Sometimes when she was particularly pleased at something she'd done, she'd squeeze my arm and I'd smile at her. I grew extraordinarily fond of her because of the warmth that I suspected was trapped behind the fear. I had my own grim memories of childhood and my own knowledge of terror.

Maggie was growing more troubled. 'Do you think you could pretend you were my doctor or priest or something?

I need to talk and tell someone how awful I'm getting. I only think about myself. I'm very selfish.'

I didn't say anything. Selfishness was certainly one of Maggie's traits, but it didn't describe her completely.

'Look, I shouldn't lecture you,' I said after a time. She started to cry at the gentleness in my voice and I felt so sorry for her and so helpless in the face of her misery.

My husband was convinced that Maggie spent her life playing to the gallery and suggested that lack of an audience would be a marvellous physician.

Next time I saw her, she was brittle and cheerful and quite unwilling to discuss our last meeting. She twittered on about some daffodils Tish had planted. I wondered inwardly about what causes our rhythms.

'How's Iain?' I asked.

'Iain? He's so busy being well balanced that he hasn't time to pay attention to me. Most of what goes on in the world just passes men by. Unless they have to go to war or something like that.'

'Are you blind?' I said shortly. 'Don't you think being responsible for Tishy has changed Iain? You're very unfair.'

'He never makes the slightest effort to find out what's bothering me. If he notices that I'm getting ready to tear my hair out, he makes some profound manly remark like "Pull yourself together, darling". That's what I call helpful advice.'

'And do you ever notice if he's ready to pull *his* hair out? Or is anguish an exclusively female affliction?'

'I thought you were on my side. I'm in despair because I

realise he no more understands what I'm thinking than he knows what's going on in the mind of the zebra in the zoo.'

She began to drop hints that set me thinking that she and Iain weren't sleeping together any more but of course that's just speculation on my part. I know that they were both unhappy. Once Maggie told me that she wanted to take Tish and go back to Minnesota. She said she couldn't bear it any longer.

'What's the point of a marriage like ours?' she asked me one day. 'We can't talk to each other – we've nothing to say any more. We're just worn out with fighting.'

She talked too much and said too many things and later she was punished for it. All the things she said nailed that marriage into its coffin. Still, no doubt at the Final Judgement, she'll be forgiven. Not even the angels would be able to resist her charm. I kept on at her until she began to cry. You see, over the years, I'd gradually turned very hard. I don't know why we didn't adopt a child of our own. On the surface, it was because John didn't want to, but I know that I hid gratefully behind his objections. I've always been easily frightened and I was too timid to look into the future with an unknown child.

But Maggie pulled me towards her as she did everyone. I still remember the hours we spent talking, talking, talking – about everything.

'Do you know we had Iain's boss and his wife to dinner last night,' she said, 'and his wife, she had to flick some dust off the chair before she could sit down and I thought Iain was humiliated but I was furious. It's not necessary to de-fluff chairs in other people's houses, is it?'

'Not usually,' I laughed, 'but in your house …' She threw a hair-brush at me. 'You see,' I added, 'not everybody keeps their hair-brush in the kitchen.'

She laughed too. 'OK. You know me better than anybody. I thought I'd show off and make jugged hare. Not a good idea. We all got hysterics finally, because the meat was so tough it kept sliding all over our plates. It was our guest who said Uncle first. After he put his knife and fork down, we all said Thank God and surrendered too. I had to throw it out. Then we had lemon meringue pie, and I'd done something frightful there too. For some reason I'd halved all the quantities – I think I only had two eggs – but I forgot to halve the sugar, so it was foul – I've never tasted anything so sugary. So that was uneatable. Then the coffee – I suppose I let it boil over – it was bitter – especially after the lemon meringue pie – and I couldn't drink it though the rest made a gallant effort. There was most dreadful silence amidst the sipping. Then our guest made some long-winded and sup-posedly humorous remark about how his wife was usually in a bad mood after a dinner party because she was jealous of the other woman's cooking, but she'd be in a good mood tonight – ha, ha – something like that. His wife tried to kick him under the table, but she got me instead. Iain was – as you can imagine – apoplectic later.'

'We can't all be good at everything, but it must have been hard for Iain if he cared about his boss's opinion,' I said, trying to be fair.

She giggled. 'I'm good at everything except daily life.'

One day I was taking our rubbish out for the Thursday collection when I heard them quarrelling. I could make out

Maggie's voice, angry, derisive and mocking, much more clearly than his.

'You can at least put the garbage out even if you can't do anything else. That's a man's job. What a laugh. What kind of a man are you?'

He was flushed when he came out carrying the bin, realising, of course, that I'd overheard, and so I averted my eyes as I said, 'Good morning.'

'You must have heard.'

I looked at him and felt such overwhelming pity for his shame and embarrassment.

'How much did you hear?' he persisted.

'Come back to my house,' I said. 'John's gone to the hospital.' He followed me into the kitchen. 'Let me get you some coffee,' I continued, and put on the kettle.

'I guess you heard it all.'

'Oh, Iain.' I switched off the kettle. 'I'm so sorry.'

And before I understood properly what I was doing, I had kissed him, very close to the mouth.

'I'm sorry,' I repeated.

He gave me a violent hug and left. This peculiar encounter was never mentioned by either of us again, but I did thereafter find myself bringing his name sympathetically into my conversations with Maggie.

Well, naturally, me taking Iain's part so often put a strain on my friendship with her. It was certainly true that Maggie had flaws. She had an equal measure of charm and faults and I began to notice every fault. I thought, of course, that she wasn't intelligent enough for Iain – that he needed someone with brains and obviously she must be boring to talk to. I began to feel sorry for Iain. She was so flamboyant; I thought, he needs someone quiet and perceptive. Someone who isn't sparkling herself but only cares about making him happy. I felt so sorry for him because he was clearly ill matched with Maggie. When you consider all those things she'd said about him, it was obvious that he must be very unhappy. Someone ought to console him. I had started out disliking him and making fun of him but my feelings were changing. He began to remind me of a confused and vulnerable puppy dog. Being next-door neighbours we saw a lot of each other over the garden fence and every Friday night he used to drive me the fifteen miles to Oxford where we'd each do our week's grocery shopping – Maggie would give Iain a list and John couldn't be bothered coming. I began to have odd fancies.

My friendship with Iain progressed very rapidly – and then stopped dead. It went so far – and not an inch further. I had assumed that things would drift along until I put a stop to them (I, of course, had no intention of allowing anything serious to happen), but I'd reckoned without Iain himself putting on a set of invisible brakes. And when I realised that nothing was going to happen for me to put a stop to – why, I'm ashamed to say – I was overcome with rage and humiliation. Then I never wanted to see him again. I told John I was sick of doing the Friday night shopping, that he could go with Iain instead. I was as frosty as possible every time I saw him. And I wanted him to say 'What's wrong?' so I could tell him, but he didn't. He knew he couldn't possibly get involved with me, being my next-door neighbour, so he began to draw back gently. That's what I

38

told myself. There was no real reason for my pride to be hurt because nothing had ever been said and after a few weeks I was friendly and cheerful again, but more distant. It took me months to get on my feet again, to regain my balance. And then, except for the tiniest bit of formality between us, you wouldn't have known.

After this humiliation, I noticed that he and Maggie seemed to have entered a more pleasant stage in their relationship. They began to go out to dinner and have parties and go to concerts. People were always in their house. It certainly looked like a happy, successful marriage. They kept inviting children of Tishy's age over, trying to force her into social activity, but Tish was an intensely solitary child and to know what she was thinking was impossible. They kept very busy, I think, to avoid any reflection about what was happening. But all along there was a darkness under it. I think Maggie still, in her heart, wanted a separation, but that's never easy. Every time she mentioned her thoughts to me, I pointed out that she had to think of Tishy.

'It wouldn't be fair to Tish,' I said self-righteously.

As for the child, she played marbles and hopscotch and didn't like school very much but she put up with it. They pushed her into all sorts of clubs, into Brownies and into music lessons. She smiled agreeably and shone at nothing.

'We went to see her teacher last night,' Maggie said over coffee one afternoon, 'to find out if there was any way we could *help* her. We thought if there's something we're not doing that we could be doing – I mean, we'd never forgive ourselves if she missed her chance. We feel it's so important – she's seven now, if she misses out, it could ruin her life. It's a vicious circle once they get discouraged and we want to break it before it gets started.'

'Leave the child alone,' I answered. 'She's got her life – and she's part of your life – books, holidays, talk around the table –' I stopped. Family meals can be sadistic occasions when individuals are trapped by the need to eat.

'What do you talk about – around the table?' I asked.

She stammered. 'We ask her about her day at school. We try to get her to talk, I mean, she'd never say anything if we didn't ask. She sits like a bump on a log. We've given her everything, holidays, clothes, books – we take her to children's plays and concerts, we play Scrabble with her, and none of it seems to show. Other kids, they're bright and alert. Don't misunderstand me – we love her for what she is. I don't want a genius for a child. It's just – Iain went to university and I think I'm quite bright. How did we get her?'

Most parents in that position pretend it is their child's own welfare which is bothering them: not many admit that they dislike the reflection which they see of themselves in their child.

'You're truthful,' I said.

'Sure, and I'm a lousy mother too. I'm so ashamed. I'm disappointed, you see.'

'Maybe she's not too keen on you as a mother either,' I said. 'Maybe she was hoping for something better too. She's got as many feelings as you have, you know.'

'I never thought of it like that. Surely children just accept what they've got, take it for granted?'

'I was trying to make you see it from a different angle. Of

course she accepts you just as you are. Might be nice if you could do the same for her.'

Tishy started coming into my classroom after school probably because I used to stop for a while after the children had gone and make myself a snack. She never said much, just 'Thank you for the biscuits,' and then she'd leave. This went on for weeks.

One day I began telling her about my own childhood and she listened, very still. I told her about the foster homes and the children's institutions and the couple who had almost adopted me, but how I hadn't been lively and sparkling enough. It was the first time in my life I'd told anyone, including John.

'If I wasn't theirs, do you think Mum and Dad would have adopted me?'

'Yes,' I lied.

'Yes, of course they would,' she agreed, and had another biscuit.

All this time, Iain and Maggie were edging towards a decision to separate. When the bough breaks, the cradle will fall ...

'You owe it to Tish,' I said to Maggie. 'You brought her into the world; now you must give her a mother and a father.'

'You can't begin to understand,' she would complain. 'I don't see how it gives Tish a stable home to hear us shouting at each other all the time.'

But they set their teeth and decided they were going to endure each other. Both products of Puritan, Mid-West America, they felt in some vague way that disaster would be precipitated by cutting the marital cord. Partly because they couldn't talk to each other, they did more play-acting than was advisable. Maggie set out to be Happy Wife and Good Mother, and Iain aimed for Hearty, Concerned Father. That damages truth beyond repair. They had only one quarrel of any magnitude – something about not ironing him a shirt – you know, the usual symbolic triviality. He knocked out one of her teeth. Yes, Iain, the Boy Scout. No, I can't account for it. It doesn't square with anything else he ever did. She got a new tooth and they went on holiday together. When they returned, things seemed much better. While they were away, I took an overdose but all that happened was that I coughed up some blood.

What is a child's happiness worth, or is it beyond valuation? I wonder at what point the character sets, jells? or is it forever fluid? No, at some early time, a profound experience enters the soul and brands it leaving the owner forever – what? – determined – frightened – crafty – secretive – self-confident – anxious – single-minded? Those of us who regularly watch children growing up have seen it. I don't know why it makes me sad to think of it, this unfolding from a few genes into the complex system that the seven-year-old is. But I do always feel obscurely affected when I think of growth and change in children. Two characteristics of Tish's which I observed from about the age of three were perceptiveness and an overpowering sense of failure. As soon as she had any personality at all, those two traits shone through. It's difficult to know what to do when the gods hand you that. What moral philosophers don't understand is that most of us can do no more than tread water in our efforts not to sink: it is given only to geniuses to swim. I think of her often in that cot by the Chianti lamp, gurgling and cooing and smelling her baby smells, not knowing the griefs which were to come. So she grew and lost the blankness of babyhood, lost the absolute assurance of protection, began to look out for herself, processes which are inevitably hardening and diminishing. Some children have a natural talent for self-reliance: they are the ones who dart ahead. Tishy held back, cautiously testing each step. Such an attitude is not necessarily foolish, but those children are not picked out for praise by their elders.

One looks back at those days and wonders at their uneventfulness, at the quiet rhythm of boredom. It is the substance of life, grey time rippling over one, a condition of blessedness which we are too stupid to understand or be grateful for.

She began to sleep poorly when she was about nine years old, waking often in the night in terror at her dreams.

'I'm afraid to go to sleep at night. It's the dark and the quiet.'

'I know,' I said. 'I don't like waking up in the dark either.'

'Oh, it's not waking up,' she said, impatiently. 'I'm afraid that when I'm asleep somebody's going to get me. I saw on television how somebody was stabbed in their sleep by a man coming through the window and I keep looking at the curtains blowing and wondering when I'm going to see a hand or a foot come through and I'm afraid to close my eyes in case suddenly a knife comes into me. And I'm afraid to go into any room at night that doesn't have the curtains drawn because I'm afraid that somebody's outside, quietly watching, that they can see me and I can't see them.'

In the heart of a child lies coiled the snake from the Garden of Eden.

'People get killed all the time,' she went on.

'You aren't worried about dying?' I laughed.

'No, but I'm afraid of being hurt.'

I remembered her mother and me crouching by the fire, sick with fear at the thought of impending childbirth.

'I'm going to have a needle next week because Mum thinks I might be anaemic and I'm scared of that.'

'The needle'll just hurt for a minute but it's to help you feel better.'

She shook her head.

I don't want to give the impression that she was a total wimp. One day she came bounding over to my classroom to show me short division which she'd finally mastered. Another time, with wild excitement, she gave me running instalments of the story of the Norman Conquest. Her teacher put on a play with the children and Tishy had a small speaking part. She had to say, ''Tis ten thousand men, sire, the enemy force, sire.' A bit hackneyed, but there it was. School plays tend to be like that, especially when they're written by teachers.

''Tis ten thousand men, sire, the enemy force, sire. You have to say it slowly, so the King understands and is afraid. Slow and loud, that's what Mr Sparling says, so the audience understands too. Clive Harris *trembles* when I say it. I'm the most important person on the stage when I say it.'

And I'm the most important person on the stage when I take a boning knife or a codeine bottle …

'I'm so excited about it,' she continued. But then she looked sad. 'Did you know that William the Conquerer wouldn't let the English have Harold's body after he was killed, but the lady who loved him – her name was Edith – stole his body and gave him a proper burial?'

'No, I didn't,' I said.

'Mr Sparling told us. I can see it if I close my eyes: a secret burial with gold cloth around the body and holy music, but soft so the Normans wouldn't hear it, and bells and priests. It must have been so beautiful and so sad.'

She was touching history.

'She seems to be doing much better this term,' Maggie told me. 'I knew she'd finally come out of her shell. Some children are just late developers,' she added happily. 'Mind you, she's got a lot of lost time to make up for. But I think she's got a bit of backbone now. She's trying at last, thank God. We had a very good report from the teacher when we went for our interview last night.'

Tish was the kind of child who is hardest of all to teach. I was never her class teacher, but I did quite a bit of remedial work with her in the evenings – or tried to. A sick smile was sometimes all you'd get out of her when you were tearing yourself apart to make her relax and open up. She just kept saying 'Yes' and trying to please without understanding what was wanted. I nearly cried. Because unless you can put your thoughts into words, they don't exist. For during the period of time that you are blank, you're not growing any more – you're paralysed. I know because that is what happened to me.

It was when she was eleven that she discovered that she wanted to paint, like Maggie. She had a very different talent from Mag's. Her mother's paintings were wistful, infinitely tenuous, reaching out for something, you didn't know what – purple, blue, black, all her paintings were dying.

But Tish's pictures were violent – all the things she didn't say were on the canvas. Bright yellows and reds – so much bloodstained red, frenzied and grisly pictures. Her paintings looked uncontrolled as though she had too much to say having stagnated for so many years. But really, she painted with extreme caution.

It was odd, the different ways they set about their work. Maggie used to slap the paint on carelessly, wildly, spontaneously. Whereas Tishy, with her gory, gaudy images – she'd dab a spot of bright red on, a tiny speck at a time, bit by bit she'd build up her scene of carnage with infinite deliberation.

It was when she learned to paint that she learned to read properly; the two appeared to be connected. It was as though once she had released all that anger within her, then she was ready to read. But she did not learn to relax in conversation. I think both Maggie and Iain used to regard her with amused resignation – that she was their solemn child. She never did talk easily. Or rather, she talked in spasms followed by months of monosyllables.

Maggie was so transparent that it was comical. No, I'm not condemning her. For anyone barren like me it's impossible to gauge the intensity of a mother's involvement in her only child and the complex emotions which linger around this only child. There was an uneasiness and instability in that family. They all hung together like a saturated solution – one tiny drop more and there'd be a crisis, the solution would precipitate, you got the feeling there'd be an irreversible change. And I just stood there, waiting for it.

It's so hard to tell where you are in the rhythm of life: you may think you're dropping, only suddenly to be raised. This divine throwing of dice sometimes gets too much for me and I stop with a kind of *petit mal* of the soul. Or putting it another way, I indulge in a spot of attention-seeking self-dispatch.

I think many marriages are held by a thread for their entire duration and it's chance alone whether or not that thread breaks. 'Such an excellent mystery.' That's how the Prayer Book describes marriage, but I'm sure there wasn't a trace of irony in Cranmer. It was all so sad, the sadness of solitude, of not ever really knowing what's going on in another person's heart. Whatever happens, there's pain. When your child dies, he just dies – final. There's no leading up to it, a step at a time. If you know that, nothing can ever again hurt you, nothing can ever again take you by surprise. Stop. Stop. Stop. I am spinning out of control again.

I suppose the trouble had more to do with the fact that Iain had always had a clear concept of who he was and what he hoped to accomplish, whereas Maggie was like a weather-vane, turning every way with the latest wind. Iain was ambitious; he'd hoped for a university career. He became a local councillor just before Maggie met Simon. Dead-earnest Iain was and yet for all my sneers such an honest man who cared about Tishy. My sneers have something to do with the fact that he rejected me. It still hurts a little, all these years later. Yet I do feel ill-defined pity for people who deliberately set out to accomplish things. You should either live in the richness of the day or, if you're very lucky, you might be taken up, have your entire life conscripted into the service of God without so much as a by-your-leave. But, to me, there's something mildly ludicrous about making sensible plans. The gods, I think, don't like it.

On the surface, he seemed so much stronger than Maggie, but later on he bellowed a lot because he was afraid of losing control. Some people are noisy when they are frightened and I remember him shouting and ranting and looking bewildered. We all thought, Poor Iain, which enraged him even more.

I'm sorry, dear Reader, that I've jumped all over the place, interweaving bits that are years apart and leaping from character to character, but without fragmented vision I cannot see the story whole. Now that we have reached this stage, I promise that I'll keep the rest of the narrative straightforward and chronological. I hope that will be satisfactory.

Chapter 2

We have now reached September 1973. Tishy was ten years old and Maggie was thirty. I shall try to keep time tidy from now on.

It was a peculiar year. Maggie was finishing off her certificate course at the college of education and I had joined her there for one year in order to get my B.Ed. All those essays – 'The Value of the Michaelmas Sociology Course to me' and 'Discuss the Problem of the Teacher's Authority in the Classroom' – strange things like that. I hadn't written essays for fifteen years and I couldn't think what to say about the problem of authority. Was authority a problem? I wondered.

Maggie thought it was wonderful; she said at last she felt a person in her own right. She kept telling me that women were systematically down-trodden by men and not regarded as real people, only reflections of others. Mind you, I've often thought the same but to hear Maggie say it – Maggie who used her female charm for everything from avoiding parking tickets (Oh, Awf-ficer, is *that* what a double yellow line means? Good heavens! When will we Americans ever learn? I think you English bobbies are jess wunnerful!! – and giggling and winking and fluttering away as though she had a speck of grit in her eye) – everything from that to getting some besotted male student to write her college essays – to hear Maggie complain petulantly of sexual discrimination was a source of delight and amusement.

'Maggie, you wouldn't have got into this college in the first place if it weren't for your charming female giggle. You can't add and you can't spell.'

But Maggie, as in everything else in her life, wanted to have it both ways. She needed worship and adoration but as soon as she got it she complained that her intellect was not being taken seriously. She was not competent at anything because she'd never had to try. All her life a dazzling smile or a tear-filled eye had immediately rescued her from the slightest difficulty.

'There's no point in talking about sexual equality,' I said. 'If your every action springs from the hope of sexual inequality – the hope that you'll get something for nothing. Like an essay written in return for telling some dolt how clever he is. You have to admit, Mag, that a smile is cheap payment for a thousand words, that he might reasonably have put the price up. And how much will you pay for your big essay at the end of the year and if not, why not?'

'Polly ...!'

'Look, as you grow older and get wrinkles you'll find that a sweet smile will buy less and less – it will be given right back to you just as sweetly. You really can't have it both ways – if you're going to be a feminist, it'll be a long and painful process because you're going to have to learn how to do things for yourself – things you've always handed to a man with a helpless sigh and a shrug of the shoulders.'

She considered this and pouted. She no longer complained to me that her talents went unrecognised because she was a woman, but Iain and Tish were given to understand that she was little more than their servant, meek, underrated, long-suffering and without any chance of bringing her light from beneath the bushel. Unfortunately, they both laughed. This would bring Maggie to the edge of hysteria.

'I am not an object,' she declaimed. 'I am a person in my own right.'

Iain made up a song which he used to sing in order to irritate her:

> I'm not a spider or a bumble-bee,
> I am a person so listen to me,
> I'm not a crumpet nor a bit of skirt,
> I am a mortal readily hurt,
> Neither a piano nor a double bass,
> I am a part of the human bloody race,
> I'm not a quasar nor an achondrite,
> I am a woman in my own true right,
> Just call me bitter and twisted too,
> Boo hoo hoo hoo, boo hoo hoo hoo.

There were four more verses. I began to sympathise with Maggie.

As I said, she enjoyed her three years at the college. I, on the other hand, found my one year there totally irksome. At the age of thirty-seven, I did not take kindly to being warned by the college chaplain about the dangers of sexual promiscuity nor to being told by a youth of twenty, who seemed to be Head Boy, to come straight to him if I had any private worries.

I felt that I knew better than most of the lecturers. I had just come from a classroom, you see, while they hadn't had to constantly melt down and reshape their theories, year by year, to fit each fresh lot of thirty-five. They didn't understand how real children force expediency. So I can't help smiling slightly when I'm told by a college lecturer that I ought to have six children frying pancakes on the stove in the corner, four others timing themselves with stop watches to see how fast they can run the length of the classroom (that's maths), another dozen in rapt absorption writing poetry based on their recent school trip to London (and, miraculously, needing no help with ideas or spelling), six more weighing the contents of the sandpit directly in the path of a small group engaged in 'free play with water'. The rest should be working on a musical composition using cigar tins filled with pebbles and stones beaten rhythmically upon the floor. As for me – oh yes, I am to be found sitting in a rocking chair with a child in my lap, the two of us chuckling warmly together over the pictures in his story book. Never mind, it was pleasant meeting new people, even if we were all teachers.

When Maggie went out on teaching practice, I envied her control of some of these young louts of fourteen and fifteen and her ability to get them enthusiastic. She was superb. I remembered the time, many years before, when I was first training to be a teacher and I had had to go into a secondary modern as a student. They crucified me. Yet Maggie, who gave all the outward signs of incompetence, had the bright

52

ideas and they responded to her. It's a pity that she didn't get into a secondary school as an art teacher where she wouldn't have had to worry about lowest common denominators or how to spell 'Arctic'. She loved her three years at college because everyone, both there and at the schools where she did her practices, they all adored her. I think those were the three happiest years of Maggie's life.

What I remember most about my year at the college is the noise and clamour and how disappointed I was at this. I'd been hoping for a quiet time, a vacuum in which to reflect upon what I was doing with my life but with all the flurry of that year, serious thought evaporated. I lurched from one empty lecture to the next. Normally, I get up early and try to set aside a private time for facing the day but I was too jangled that year.

I injudiciously told Maggie about my solitary time first thing in the morning and, my goodness, she laughed. There were many things I resented about Maggie but I particularly hated the way she pitied me. This was the most private thing I'd ever told her.

'I don't see why you laugh,' I said stiffly.

'Well, it hasn't done you much good in terms of reducing stress, has it?'

'No, you're right there,' I laughed. When you have been hurt, you don't compound your injury by telling the perpetrator.

There was a pause and then she said, 'I think Mr Culler is very attractive, don't you?'

I raised an eyebrow.

'And clever,' she went on.

'And he's bewitched by you,' I responded.

She protested charmingly.

'However, don't let Iain hear you dribble on.'

'Don't lecture me. Anyhow, Iain takes everything so seriously,' she sighed. And you take nothing seriously, I thought.

'I lecture you because I care about you,' I said. 'The world is at your feet – don't underestimate that. You're one of the luckiest people on earth. Be grateful for the glories heaped upon you. You have a husband and a child and your painting and skill with teaching and all your charm – don't be greedy.'

These thoughts take one back and back, into the roots of behaviour, and I wondered what deprivation she had suffered early on to make her so desperate for admiration. There must be some universal longing to go back, back before the Fall, back into the freshness of innocence. That is probably why one's heart contracts at the sight of a young child. We can only wait until we get to the other side of the grave to understand it all. Those things which are outwardly contradictory, such as the greediness of the lovely Maggie Miles – when the veil is lifted, suddenly the outline will not be blurred, everything will be sharp and clear and we will cry out in joy and surprise that we had not understood it earlier. I hope.

Anyhow, she went through her three years at the college falling in love with every presentable male in sight, getting them all to do her little favours. I remember one night when Iain, rather bitter, came over to see me when Maggie was out at a college party. My husband was at the hospital, working late. This is usual for him.

'Maybe she'd rather I just left and then she could do what she liked. I'd hate to cramp her style.'

'You know that basically she's completely faithful to you.'

'She'll go too far,' he said furiously, 'and then enough will be enough.'

I thought of the troop of men who followed his wife everywhere at the college. It was only a matter of time …

'You'll never stop forgiving her,' I said sadly.

'But I think you're right,' he added, ignoring my last remark. 'I think she still loves me in her own funny way.'

'Have a drink,' I said.

I thought there is such a short distance between us. He looked tired and strained, the lines of his mouth set crookedly. We sat down on the sofa with a gin and tonic. And I wanted Iain Miles more than anyone before or since.

I love you, I love you.

'Yes, she loves you,' I said.

There was a knock on the door and Maggie bounced in. She'd been drinking but just enough to put brightness into her cheeks.

'Hi, you two. Can I make myself some coffee? I went home first, but when you weren't there, I thought you'd be here, so I came straight over. You missed a good party. There was Eddy Culler and Christie and Al Farmer and Mark and that drama chap. It was ever so funny. Al Farmer had us in stitches. I wish I could have stayed all night.' She shook back her mane of thick long black hair and jumped on the sofa and sat down at one end with her feet tucked under her.

'I think we'd better get home, Mag,' Iain said. He tried to sound stiff, but he was yielding by the moment.

My husband came in at about three in the morning. You have to take what you can get and he was no doubt thinking the same.

I don't know what Iain and Maggie said to each other that night, but for a few months afterwards her flirtations stopped. Why was she not satisfied? I asked her. After all, Iain still worshipped her and not many husbands feel that way after more than ten years of marriage. Certainly not mine. But then John and I have a strange and atypical marriage though one which, oddly enough, accommodates us both. I think.

'You want to know why I'm not satisfied?' she answered. 'I can't help it. It's a sense of power, that intelligent, sophisticated men are made wobbly by looking at me. I know that Iain's worth ten of any of these twerps at the college – but that's what attracted me to Iain in the first place: his brains. I was proud that a man like that wanted me.'

'You are lucky,' I said wistfully. 'Because everybody falls for you, Mag, and you can take your pick. You could go into a room and look at every man in turn and every one of them would fall silent, stop what they were doing, and look back at you.' I knew all this because I'd seen it, over and over again. 'The trouble with you, though,' I went on, 'is that you want more and more. You're never satisfied. First Iain, then one after another, every man you meet. And is Eddy Culler the latest, or is it Al Farmer? When will you stop? One day you'll find a man who treats you with contempt – and he'll break you because you can't bear not being adored.'

But during her entire time at the college she continued to go to parties, parties where she flirted with admiring males. And her essays got written.

The four of us went out to dinner one night.

'We're thinking of Tish's future now,' Iain was saying. 'It's early days but one can't start thinking about these things too soon. It's obvious that her talents are artistic rather than academic.'

Parenthood is pitiful. John and I both looked at our plates while Iain trailed off.

'It's like this,' Maggie explained. She stopped and I knew exactly what she was thinking.

'When you get to heaven, there's only one soul you have to account for and that's your own,' I said. 'You spend too much time agonising over Tish. She'll grow up soon enough.'

Maggie turned scarlet.

'Of course parents have a duty to look after their children's interests,' Iain said impatiently. 'Loving implies keeping a look-out for opportunities. If we don't do it for her, who will? And if that isn't loving, what is?'

'Just loving.'

'Loving a child implies pushing her ahead.'

'What utter tripe,' I snarled between my teeth. 'You're doing it for yourself, so you can say to other parents, Look at my child who has done so much better than your child. That's because my child had a head-start with better genes.'

'So you think we're pushy parents,' Iain went on relentlessly. 'You always think everything is so simple. What you don't understand – and it's because you haven't got children of your own – is the strength of our involvement. Having a child is like having a second chance in life, and you're determined not to make a hash of it. Every parent worth his salt wants to give his child a good start. What exactly's wrong with that?'

I could not reply of course. John remarked upon the delicious mayonnaise, unusual in a restaurant. I nodded silently. Maggie told a funny story about the last time she'd attempted mayonnaise and how many egg yolks she'd used up before it came out right. You'd think I'd be used to it by now: my inability to produce a viable child. For some reason, Iain had more power to hurt me than anyone else. *a large squashed head a purple face* I began nervously to rub my wine glass back and forth across my hand. The glass had a slight chip in it and within moments I was bleeding profusely. To this day, I have a small white scar on the back of my left hand …

One wonders when a child is shaped. What had happened in the time between ten months and ten years to make Tishy's eyes so sad? At the age of ten years, Tishy bore the immense knowledge that she was a disappointment and this blotted out the hope of gaining other, more liberating knowledge.

'What's wrong?' I asked one day over biscuits at my house.

She shrugged and went on eating. I should have let her be, but I persisted. She arched her neck and curled her lip and her eyes were pulled together by the troubled furrows on her brow. She looked ugly for just a moment. She shrugged again.

58

'Not so good?' I went on.

But then she was crying and sobbing convulsively. She made terrible noises and went an unnerving colour while her nose dribbled and her eyes swelled up. Maggie, long ago, had mastered the art of crying prettily, but she had not passed the skill on. She tried to say that she was all right but she couldn't get the words out. Then she put her head on my table and sobbed and sobbed. I put my arms around her and squeezed hard. I was crying too, and my tears were wetting her hair. She calmed down eventually of course, and I suggested that she go and wash her face. I stared glumly at the wall while awaiting her return. But when she came back, still looking dreadful, I said nothing because I knew that I was powerless.

Tell me now, what would you have done? Of course I should have investigated, found out what was troubling her. But even if she'd had the means to unravel her misery in words, I doubt if I would have understood. Of course, all children cry and feel misery and frustration, but the memories are wiped out by time. We forget. 'You want to protect them.' That's what parents say, isn't it? When they look at their infants and see into the future, there is a sudden rushing desire that nothing shall change, that it will somehow be possible to keep those promises to protect. So many times I have thought of her in that cot by the Chianti lamp, looking out through those velvet brown eyes, innocent of pain.

Then, as Maggie had hoped, Tish seemed to settle. She came over to see me less and less. I thought it was probably that she was outgrowing her need for comforting and I told myself that it was a good sign. Anyhow, I was busy writing my end-of-year essay and Maggie was busy organising someone else to write hers. Iain kept coming to see me from time to time.

'Problems?' I asked one day as he seemed to be in a sulking mood.

He stretched his legs and smiled unhappily. 'I have one huge problem called Maggie, but other than that I'm fine. God knows what I'm going to do, though. If He does know, He seems to have forgotten to tell me.' I began to feel as though I were invisible. 'So I ask you, Polly Macdonnell – what is the meaning of life? I can't think of anyone better to ask. You know the answer to every other bloody question.'

He wasn't very drunk, but I was cautious all the same. From my early years, I've had enough *in vino veritas* to last me a lifetime.

'That isn't true, as you are perfectly aware,' I said.

He started to laugh. 'You think I'm drunk and I wish I were. I'm sure alcohol makes the days slip down easier. No, here am I, just turned thirty-four and what is there for me in life? I married Maggie and I thought, Here now, we'll do something great together. I'll conquer the world with Mag beside me, thought I. But Maggie wanted to conquer both me and the world, and her fire, instead of warming me, it now burns me. So what of all these great ambitions? What world precisely am I going to conquer? No, it's conquered me.'

I was, as you can imagine, highly embarrassed and uncomfortable, full of uneasiness. I didn't know what to reply.

'I know what you're thinking,' he said, frightening me. 'You have contempt for me that I should be telling you this.

But I want to talk and I have no one else to talk to,' he said earnestly.

And I'm not a threat, I thought, not to anybody.

'No,' I said slowly. 'I don't know what I could do to help.'

'I need somebody to talk to,' he replied. 'Somebody who'll keep her mouth shut. Somebody who's completely objective.' Somebody who's obviously asexual, I thought bitterly. 'I'm sorry,' he added.

'Why don't you talk to a man?' I asked.

'I wouldn't dream of it,' he said, outraged. 'Anyway, women are supposed to understand feelings and relationships,' he added with a touch of belligerence. 'But I'd forgotten. Your life's in a bit of a mess too, isn't it?'

He's not going to forgive me for seeing him weak, I thought.

'I'm Maggie's friend. It strains loyalties.'

'Do you talk about me with Maggie?'

'Of course not,' I lied. 'So I shouldn't listen to you going on about her.'

'That doesn't follow at all.'

'Yes, it does. How could a proper friendship develop between us? Friendship takes enormous slabs of time – how many afternoons like this are we going to have when we can talk at length?'

'Trust you!' he burst out laughing. 'You always were one for counting the cost before beginning to build – not once, but over and over again. You have so much scepticism and so many reservations and neuroses about everything that I don't see how you ever managed to get married in the first place. Poor John. I'm sorry,' he said and got up.

61

'I'm sorry too,' I answered quite truthfully. How odd are our animal spasms. I knew that I had wanted him to touch me, that I had wanted some sort of physical understanding. How hilarious people must appear in the eyes of the gods. I went with him to the door in a blur of painful excitement.

At the door he kissed my forehead in a friendly fashion and then he was gone. I went back into my sitting-room, looked at the fine wrinkles on my hand and disassociated myself from them. I banged the table with inarticulate rage and yelled my disapproval of the universe.

'I want to spend more time painting,' Maggie said the next time I saw her. 'Seriously, I mean.'

I've always liked Mag's paintings – soft, gentle, curving, mostly mauves and pinks. So unlike her, I've always thought. I don't understand the artistic impulse. Why do people want to write or paint or compose? It's a mystery.

'Well, that one's nice,' I said lamely.

Maggie ignored my remark and carried on. 'Inside, I'm all aswirl, all chaos, and I want to try to disentangle myself. I want a picture of my inner self that I can admire and then I'll paint what I see.'

'How impressive.'

'You're just like Iain,' she said angrily. 'I try to do something serious and all you can do is laugh. You treat me as though I were a funny little child. I'm thirty – don't you understand? – thirty. I have to find a meaning to my life. I suppose that's incomprehensible to you who were born prosaic. But I know nothing – I have to discover who I am.'

It was sometimes difficult to keep a straight face while talking to Maggie. Nevertheless, I felt uncomfortable, being linked with Iain. Born prosaic, was I? Not quite, Maggie, not quite.

'I'm sure you're very talented,' I muttered.

'It hasn't got anything to do with talent or lack of it,' she replied. 'It's that I want to find a shape to my life – some reason for living. I can't live just dragging myself from one day to the next – plod, plod – it drives me mad, Polly. I need to see the rest of the universe as having some connection with me.'

Well, that kind of talk is completely beyond me. I'm uneasy with mystic types. Because, you know, they think they're superior to the rest of us. They think they've got something we haven't got. It makes me furious, their misplaced sense of superiority. They'd have died out long ago if it weren't for us who do the work. They rely upon us. Maggie had visions of changing the world but she couldn't even change a light bulb. And what gets me is the *contempt* they feel for us. Without us, there wouldn't be a world for them to change. There, I've said it, it's off my chest. Because I loved her. I'm glad the earth turns up a few people like Maggie occasionally, spirits who burst apart because they're not satisfied with what the world has to offer. I guess both kinds are necessary. But, still, I was never able to talk to Maggie properly about her painting.

One day she invited me up to the little box room where she did her work. Everything was all over the place, cartons, canvases, paints. The chairs were overturned and the curtains askew. Tidiness did not come high on Maggie's list of priorities.

'I can't work any other way,' she answered me sharply. 'I'm not comfortable unless I pile my things around me.'

'Well ...' I said dubiously. 'It's just that there's so much, in all directions.'

She opened the curtains a little wider and I could see there was paint on the carpet. Several pictures seemed to be in various stages.

'Why don't you do just one painting at a time and then clear up?' She looked heavenward. 'I'm sure you'd get more done that way.'

'Maybe you're right. Maybe that's what I should do,' she said, sarcastically. 'It's just that I happen to like my own methods. It suits my moods better.'

I looked at her pictures again, and again I was mystified. I could see no connection whatever between Maggie and the canvases and I felt I knew her as well as anyone.

When I said that, she laughed mirthlessly. 'I paint from pain,' she said clearly. 'If you could look into these pictures, you'd understand the terror that I feel. I'd like to be able to do something positive, not just to cry out because I'm hurt, but to find a solution, in the paintings, I mean. Living with Iain, life is about the same as death – no, I don't want to discuss it – just say, I don't feel like a woman and yet it's necessary to me to be a woman. I'm chained down. That's why I paint in mauves and pinks – I can't see the bright colours. But life is more and *I want it*. But Tish ...'

'And Iain,' I said.

She sighed again. 'They hold me down, between them. How the hell am I supposed to paint surrounded by all these bloody PTA notices?'

'I don't see what the PTA has got to do with artistic vision,' I said, reasonably. 'You're not all that special, Mag. You're an ordinary woman with an inflated view of yourself. I can't begin to understand someone like you who goes around smearing oil paint on the furniture because your mind's on higher things. Can't you just compartmentalise your art? Lots of great painters have been sensible and practical. It's not Tishy's fault nor Iain's that you're held down. By marrying, by having a child, you wove yourself into your own web, you can't get out. You could have stopped at any time before you had Tish. But once past that point – no going back. You have to conform to the laws of your own nature. You want to find yourself suddenly free, without hurting a soul. The chains you talk about – they're human limbs. You stand here, solid, in this little room, 16 Whirtle Lane, Breckling-on-Thames, Oxfordshire, and your child is solid downstairs, and Iain is solid. All these whirling soulful yearnings are pretty insubstantial compared to real people you could so easily hurt. They're more important than your visions.' I was out of breath.

'You must be wrong,' she said at last. 'It can't ever be demanded that one person sacrifice herself for another. I don't know how to argue because what you say seems to make sense, but right deep in the centre of me, I don't believe it, and it's there, deep at the centre, that I have to make decisions. And everything you've said is wrong. I *know* – more than duties and responsibilities is to have some elbow room for my soul. I don't care who I hurt – no, that's not true. I do care, but I'm going to hurt them anyhow. At the very innermost point, Polly, there should be one life, one flame, one purpose, and I've found it at my centre and it's not Tishy and it's not Iain. I can account for myself before God – after all, He made me this way.'

I felt that she was profoundly uncivilised, that if there were many people like Maggie, communities would disintegrate.

'If I had a child,' I said, 'I would give up anything, anything at all for him.' That was hitting below the belt.

'No, it isn't selfishness,' she said, wearily. 'It's just a matter of doing what I'm here for. What did I procreate *for*? Just so Tishy can grow up and have a child? There must be more to it than that.'

I was going to try to nail her down. 'Every decision you make leads you inexorably to your next action. You talk as though you're living in an open field rather than in a jungle with other people and prior decisions clinging to your legs like sticky weed. That day you got pregnant, that was it. You know it too – that's why you're writhing so much.'

'How about you? How about you?' she almost screamed. 'How about you? You play games with life and death. How do you think John feels? How dare you how dare you how dare you lecture me? How dare you, how about you?' She was crying with rage.

'I don't claim to be speaking from a position of moral elevation,' I said coldly. 'Truth is truth. It does not depend upon the virtue of the messenger.'

'Oh stuff it. You can't take any criticism at all. Moment someone attacks you, up goes a fence of ice.'

The difference was that I could hurt her but she couldn't hurt me. She fell silent and I suppose she was thinking of

66

those first tiny decisions, each one so insignificant, a thousand invisible threads fastening her as securely as Gulliver. She looked very tired.

'I'm sorry,' I said, and it was part apology and part compassion.

Chapter 3

Maggie had worked with me at Breckling Primary (C of E) for three years before Simon's arrival and her subsequent collision with his life.

Derek, our Head, called me to his room one day and asked if I would have a student teacher in my classroom. Of course I didn't want one, but I generally say 'Yes' to such things and so it was on that day. I don't like fussing.

Nobody ever wants student teachers in the classroom. They sit there taking notes and turning up their noses whenever they see you doing something their tutors have warned them about. I usually send them over to the office with the register first thing in the morning so that I can bellow at the children for five minutes without hearing a gasp of disapproval in the background.

'His name is Simon Butcher.'

He was twenty-three at the time, over ten years younger than Maggie, and a thoroughly nice boy. He was unprepossessing in appearance – a large Adam's apple that shifted convulsively, a face prickly with pimples and a wispy beard that refused to grow properly – you certainly wouldn't have looked at him twice on the street. But he noticed things warmly and with humour. I don't think he was particularly intelligent; nonetheless, you just *were* comforted and strengthened when you were with him. I can't explain it any better than that except that I came to rely upon him totally during the seven weeks he was with me. I grew to care for him – no, not like Iain, not like Iain – but with a tenderness that would not have developed had he been a girl.

He was with me for two weeks before he met Maggie. It was oh, so typical, she'd asked for an unpaid leave of absence to visit a sick aunt in Bermuda for the two weeks adjoining the Michaelmas half-term. Poor Derek is like an amiable pudding and, besides, he'd always had a soft spot for Mag though I never met the man who didn't. He was cautious about calling her a liar. After all, he didn't want her to burst into outraged tears. Do you know, I don't think she was lying about the sick aunt because she was really extremely straightforward about everything. Whether she was that desperately needed by her was another matter. As she said with perfect frankness, her poor aunt wanted to see her and wasn't it fortunate that she could get a suntan in November at the same time?

'Providential. One must seize opportunities by the forelock … or is it the foreskin?'

'Be serious, Polly. Derek was very good about it. I think he's a kind man.'

' "If you get simple beauty and nought else, you get about the best thing God invents." Browning said it first. I say it every time I see you.'

She shimmered with delight. 'It's got nothing to do, nothing whatever to do with me personally. If you ever had a sick relation, I know Derek would let you have time off too. He's so kind and understanding.'

'I'm sure he is,' I said, laughing slightly. 'But then you've had more opportunities to test it than most of us.'

'My aunt is very dear to me.'

'Of course she is, my pet. I'm convinced you'd never turn your back on an old auntie who has a house in Bermuda.'

The next thing I knew, Derek asked me to come and see him in his office. He looked dreadfully uncomfortable and, of course, I assumed there'd been a complaint by a parent. What was it, I wondered. Too harsh with her child? Not severe enough? Child unhappy, doesn't understand what I'm teaching? Property being stolen in the classroom and I haven't caught the thief yet? Andrew's spelling does not seem to have improved at all this year? I didn't let them have PE last week and don't I know children have to use up their energy? Child being bullied and I'm not aware of it? I felt my throat muscles tighten.

'You wanted to see me?' I could hear the gravel in my voice.

But it wasn't anything like that, thank God. It was Derek trying the old trick, trying to find out with clumsy diplomacy if Mag were competent or not. It's printed on the back of our union card that it's unprofessional to make any adverse remarks about a colleague without her being there, but it would be utterly damning to the teacher in question if you insisted that she be present before you were prepared to speak about her. You can't just refuse to reply because then the Head simply smiles and says, 'Never mind. I have my answer, thank you.'

'She's imaginative and cares a lot for the children,' I said. 'She has her own way of working which is quite effective.'

'Did you know that she'll be away for two weeks after half-term? Uuuuuh … did she mention … that she has – ah – bowed to the demands of consanguinity, as it were?'

Focusing on an oak leaf brushing against the window, I answered, 'I believe she has received a cry for help from a frail old relative and is responding by embarking upon a mission of mercy.'

'To Bermuda,' he said drily. 'An aunt,' he went on mournfully. 'Oh, Polly.'

I grinned at his appalled face.

He sighed. 'I said she could go. I know I'm an old fool, but if this gets out in the staff-room, everyone else will know it too.'

With admirable restraint, I said nothing.

'Please don't mention it to the others that her aunt lives in Bermuda. I'll announce the first day we're back after half-term that poor Mrs Miles has had to rush off suddenly to care for a sick relation – compassionate leave, we'll call it – I'll imply it's her mother, without being too definite – but I'd be very grateful if you didn't volunteer any prior knowledge and, in particular, no geographical details, please. Since she's not taking any pay for those two weeks, there'll be no problem getting a supply to cover her class.'

I promised.

That was how it came to be that Simon was in my classroom for two weeks before he met Maggie. He and I, right from the first day, worked comfortably together as equals. He was very well organised and his lessons were sensibly planned.

In what I later came to see as an inspired move, I left him

alone with the class for the first morning he was with me. I figured he'd better learn by himself how to handle Bernie Chamberlain, to say nothing of Bernie's troop of loyal servants. I learned later that they had mounted a concerted attack on him. First a dart, then low whistles, boys saying, 'Eh? eh? what? what?' when he said something. I gathered from the supply teacher next door that he'd dealt with them, one at a time, decisively. The child with the dart – Bernie, of course – was set to copying out the history of aeroplanes from the big encyclopaedia during his lunch-times. After that, they settled somewhat. He began speaking slowly and softly and they were afraid to say 'Eh?'. They had no wish themselves to acquire an encyclopaedic knowledge of the Causes of Deafness. They settled because they respected his firmness. Of course, what I did was strictly against the rules. You're supposed to huddle close to your students like a mother hen with her newly hatched chicks until you judge that they're ready for independence. Unfortunately, that gives the children time to know them and lose their awe. If the student is good, it's better to throw him in the deep end immediately so he'll lose his nervousness at once.

I returned to the classroom in the afternoon and I could see that he had won. I don't say that was all there was to it. Children like Bernie Chamberlain have to go on testing you – it's their way. But every time he tried it on, Simon was ready. He never gave an inch to insolence. Some classes are worse than others and the particular group I had when Simon was with me was rather unpleasant. But in the end he subdued Bernie by the age-old technique of giving him responsibility. He put him in charge of seeing that the other children entered and left the classroom in an orderly fashion. One had to intervene occasionally to prevent him from knocking his fellow students unconscious as a disciplinary measure, but on the whole, it worked well. He was soon hanging about, begging for extra jobs. His special treat was to be allowed to use Simon's pen-knife, a beautiful ebony object with inlaid ivory and dozens of different blades. It had his initials, S.B., on the ebony part.

'Wait till Maggie Miles comes back,' I told Simon. 'You'll love her.' I said it so lightly. I was simply looking forward to introducing them, these two people who were totally dissimilar.

'I'm getting conflicting evidence about that woman,' he said. 'Derek Lloyd and your RE teacher and the caretaker all seem devoted to the point of self-immolation. But I notice that not all the women teachers are so enthusiastic. Why do people react that strongly?'

'I don't know,' I said, puzzled. 'Some people just have that effect on others. It's a sort of charm and kindness. Maggie's terrifically kind. She's so generous, not just with money, though she's carefree with that too. She has time for you. When you're with Mag, you feel you're the most important person in the world, that she's not interested in anyone else. She goes to immense trouble to help anyone in difficulty. What else can I say? She has long black hair, and she practically dances when she walks.'

'How old is she?'

'Too old for you,' I teased him. 'She's thirty-four, but she could pass for ten years younger.'

'You haven't told me why most of the women don't like her, but I think I can guess. When will she be back?'

'Not for another week.'

'Generally, teachers don't get time off to visit sick relations, do they?'

'When they're Maggie, they do.'

One of the dinner ladies poked her head through the door in a blaze of ill humour. 'Mrs Macdonnell, could you do something about Bernie Chamberlain? He's just given one of the Infants a black eye because the poor child dropped a sweet paper on the playground. When I tried to punish him he said that Mr Butcher told him to discourage children from leaving litter.'

We burst out laughing, much to Mrs Barlow's indignation. She didn't see what was so very funny, do you mind? and it wasn't easy being a dinner controller, not if teachers didn't take their jobs seriously it wasn't an easy job at all.

'Of course we'll back you up completely,' I assured her. 'Dinner la – controllers like you are worth your weight in gold. Send him to me right away.' I looked stern.

'I'm rather fond of him,' Simon admitted when Mrs Barlow was out of hearing.

'That's because you've tamed him, more or less,' I said. 'That makes it all the more heartbreaking when things go wrong later. To read in the newspaper in ten years' time certain terrible things and to know that the good you did that child was only temporary. It makes you wonder why you ever bothered.'

'You bother for the same reason as you bother about

anything, Polly. You bother because it's important to you at the time.'

'You don't know what it's like to sweat your innards out for a child, to care and care and care, to spend hours and the payment? They forget you. Yet when they were in your class, you'd have done anything for them. It's all labour for nothing. It would be nice if they remembered you and what you tried to do for them.' *all labour for nothing to sweat your innards out for your son and care and care and care all labour for nothing*

It was one o'clock and they came streaming through the door again. Yes, I am well aware of the sort of person I am revealing myself to be. I've been through too much to hide my peevishness and I am prepared to make it perfectly clear that I am not a nice person. Many people think I'm quiet and gentle. I'm not: I rage within myself at the injuries which I have known. I can see myself as a dictator because within my heart there is such hatred at what fate has done to me. Those who have been hurt are not pleasant people. Untended wounds heal in an ugly fashion.

We had a good afternoon with the children: they were working well. I was in a happy daze being with Simon because we were yoked together so smoothly, both of us caring the same way about the children. His tutor came in later and, after he'd spoken to Simon, he told me that the working atmosphere in this classroom was one of the happiest and most eager that he'd ever seen. He was right, too, but it had more to do with Simon than either of us realised then. But that time is over and it won't return.

Simon kept coming back to the subject of the absent Maggie Miles.

'Why doesn't she learn to spell and do straightforward arithmetic then?'

'I don't know. I've asked her that myself and she always laughs and shrugs her shoulders. But she's good at other things – she's marvellous at art. And you should see them hanging on to her skirts and clustering around her as soon as she walks in. It's hard to say what makes a good teacher: they do work enthusiastically for her. They're a noisy bunch, but they quieten down as soon as she wants them to.'

'I'm looking forward to meeting the famous Maggie,' he said with a smile. 'I keep wondering what she'll be like.'

'Come on. Get the children ready. It's time for assembly.'

When we got over to the hall, I groaned. It was the hymn:

> I have seen the morning sunshine,
> I have heard the ocean's roar,
> I have seen the flowers of springtime,
> And there's one thing I am sure:
> They were all put there for us to share
> By someone so divine
> And if you're a friend of Jesus
> CLAP CLAP CLAP CLAP
> Then you're a friend of mine!
> I've seen the light
> I've seen the light
> And that's why my heart sings!
> I've known the joy

I've known the joy
That loving Jesus brings!

That hymn, not to put too fine a point upon it, makes me want to vomit. Whenever we have it I feel the day has got off to a hopeless start. Especially the CLAP CLAP CLAP bit. Yuck Yuck Yuck.

Unfortunately, the children were in a bouncy mood which didn't help. It's a lot to ask the Head to take assembly every day, but Derek does it conscientiously. Unwisely, for a Friday morning, he began talking about the concept of justice. A star-crossed venture. Even Socrates had difficulty with it, I recall. The children were uninterested in philosophic exposition and started kicking each other quietly. Bernie began practising his recently acquired skill of hawking. A new child, clearly suggestible, vomited. (Or maybe, now that I come to think of it, she was a kindred spirit responding to the hymn.) I sometimes wonder what God thinks of these acts of homage going up at 9 a.m. every Tuesday, Wednesday, Thursday and Friday from every school in the land. From Breckling (C of E), at least, the Lord gets a respite on Mondays because we collect the dinner money in lieu of assembly.

Back in the classroom, we called the register and then got down to maths. It was a good lesson: they worked hard which is always gratifying. There's no thrill quite like that of seeing a child's face light up with new understanding. It's the only kind of creativity I have. I remember that time particularly because it was the last morning before Maggie returned from Bermuda – we had three children understand something they hadn't grasped before. It was wonderful.

At break, we went over to the main building for coffee. All the teachers were in a jubilant mood. Some days the children just settle and work: it has something to do with the sunshine and calm weather. After break, we had English and they were busy writing a story about waking up to find themselves six inches tall. Subjects like that often get a spark from them: they don't seem to feel threatened by where their imagination is leading them, the way they do with more realistic stories. Of course, there are always some children who produce the same scenario over and over again, no matter what title you give them. 'How I Scored a Goal for Leeds United though I was only Six Inches Tall.' One becomes philosophic about it after a while.

'I dunno what to write about.'

You gormless child. Why don't you use your bloody imagination?

I smile tenderly and lovingly. 'Here's a six-inch ruler. Try to imagine that it's you. Now how do you start?'

Long pause. 'I dunno.'

'How do you find out that you're only six inches tall?' In the silence that follows, I imagine lying in the sun in Bermuda. 'Does it happen suddenly, or do you wake up like that?'

'I wake up.'

'How would you first notice? You're lying in bed, this size. What would you notice?'

'I dunno.'

'No, no, listen. *What would you notice about the blankets?*'

79

'They'd cover me up.'

'Do you want to be lost under the blankets in the dark?'

'Shall I start, "It was dark under the blankets when I woke up"?'

'By all means,' I say wearily. 'Whatever you like.'

'But Mrs Macdonnell ... I dunno what else to write.'

Thirty-one children are busy and cheerful, but one child has the power to make me feel a complete and utter failure.

'I want to know again ... what would you notice?' I ask mechanically.

'If I were in the classroom, I'd notice your legs. They're hairy.' The other children are reduced to muffled hysteria by his audacity. But they soon get back to work and the hour passes quickly.

Then I go and have school dinner with the children and I get into conversation with them and feel refreshed. They're so unmistakably childish over the spam fritters that all this adult fogginess is swept away. By the time they've counted the raisins in the rice pudding, I'm feeling cheerful again. Simon and I get up from our allocated tables and retire to the staff-room for coffee. By one o'clock we are both relaxed once more.

I do the teaching for the first hour: Religious Education on a Friday afternoon. One of the miracles, walking on the water. I find it difficult, but I go ahead with it grimly. I keep telling myself that it is necessary for children to know the Christian myths. The most disturbing aspect is their un-questioning credulity. Well, I tell the story and I know that, for seven-year-olds, there's no point in trying to make it symbolic. There's much to be said for not telling the children

Bible stories at all in the primary schools, but Derek won't wear that idea. So I tell them the story without much conviction and with a heavy sense of guilt at my own evasions. Simon and I spoke of it afterwards during break.

'You should be more honest, Polly,' he said severely. 'If you don't think he walked on water, then you don't tell the children that. You tell the Bible stories as a collection of fables and nothing else if that's what you believe. What difference does it make what Mr Lloyd says, or what the parents think? What matters surely is your conscience? Can't you just say that lots of people believe these stories but that you don't?'

'No, Simon, I can't. You seem to forget we've the Vicar of Breckling's kid in this class. He goes home every single Friday afternoon and recites my entire RE lesson to his Dad, word for word. You weren't here last year when a parent raised hell when I put the Bible in the fiction section in the school library. No, of course I'm joking, but it could easily happen. Remember, this is a church school.'

We had a lot of discussions during those two weeks when Maggie was in Bermuda and, in argument, Simon often won because I respected his clarity and directness. I remember how we used to discuss, over and over again, the aims of education. He had a huge panoramic vision encompassing 'the whole child', as the phrase went.

'But you haven't got time for that,' I used to say patiently. 'If you tried to deal with every need of every child, you'd have to live forever, and the children would have to stop growing and changing while you raced from one to the other tending to each child's multiple facets. You must have priorities. It isn't possible to say, "I'm attending to the whole child." Of course I understand that a person can't concentrate if something's upsetting him and you have to try to remove the obstruction before he can settle and learn. Of course I know that. But that's background awareness. The day is too short and there are too many children crowding around you to have fuzzy aims. You'd end up teaching nothing of value. Moral education, emotional education, social education – start aiming for those things and you teach nothing at all. You're paid to teach reading, writing and arithmetic. If you start concentrating on "the whole child", you'll wake up one morning and realise they haven't learned a damn thing all year.'

'You're wrong. You don't have to consciously tick off fifty categories for each child,' he said. 'But what you do have to do when you're teaching maths is to be aware that there's more to that particular child than his ability to add.'

'Of course. But you're paid to teach him to add.'

Anyhow, we often talked like that sometimes quite literally for hours – we'd begin nattering at three-thirty at the end of school, I'd finally ask him home for supper with us and we'd still be contradicting each other at one in the morning when he'd at last leave. I can't remember who won, but we were each passionate in defence of our own theories.

'You have only one life,' I would say. 'You have to be careful about the decisions that you make.' It occurred to me that Simon did not know my background. I assumed that he supposed that I was mature and well balanced, which shows how unobservant I was.

82

I remember the last hour of that last Friday afternoon before Maggie returned from Bermuda. We had discussed the point of education all during that break and I said, 'I'm whacked. Let's take it easy till home-time.'

'You mean, let's use an audio-visual aid,' he said, conspiratorially.

We chose the radio music programme and the speaker was teaching the children a song which will fret me for the rest of my life, a shallow little melody but one which will not go away. Even now, it scrapes through my sleep and my waking hours. It reminds me, again and again, of my days with Simon before Maggie returned. 'One more river to go.' It carries with it the distant aches, yearnings, echoes of unproductive time.

> One more river,
> One more river to go,
> One more river,
> And that's the River of Jordan!

We sat in the glow of the paraffin heater on that bright, undefiled November afternoon and I was so comfortable and warm. I no longer needed to argue with Simon. The sun shone in through the west window and a column of golden dust floated around the classroom. 'One more river to go.' I felt weightless in time, perhaps because of the knowledge that that particular kind of happiness would soon be finished.

I went home and spent the weekend doing the usual things: washing and ironing and shopping. I always had a faint sense of boredom when Maggie was not in Breckling. All my life, I have been too dependent upon other people.

I was washing the kitchen floor when I heard Maggie's taxi arrive. It was my instinct to dash out and fling my arms about her, but I told myself that she wanted to be alone with Iain and Tish first. I polished the pots and pans and then the silverware. After dinner, I sat down with an enormous basket of mending. I remembered, when I had been in hospital after Timothy's birth, when I had started talking to myself, how the nurses had given me needle and thread and a bag of torn linen to keep me from brooding. To this day, I cannot look at a pile of mending without faint stirrings of grief. Then, because I was nervous and irritable, I made a pan of fudge. Suddenly there was a knock on the door and there was Maggie in all her intensity of life.

'Mag!' I cried, and hugged her tightly.

'Do you like my suntan?'

'You'll have a hard time accounting for it in the staff room. There have been comments while you've been away, lassie. That's the trouble with you, Mag – you make people jealous.' I was so glad to see her. Two weeks had seemed like a century. 'Do be careful what you say when you come back.'

'I wouldn't dream of keeping it secret,' she retorted.

'Of course you'll tell them.' It was true – she seldom lied. 'I've tried to imply that it's been a painful and harrowing time for you.'

She laughed now.

'Don't push your luck, Mag,' I said quietly.

'Don't look so worried. I'll go into the staff-room, say, "Ha! Ha! Ha! Guess where I've been?" – then I won't tell them. You've heard of people whose hair has gone white with grief overnight? I'll say that sorrow has turned my skin brown. All right, all right,' she sighed. 'I'll be good.'

'Glad to hear it,' I said. 'Oh, I've got a simply first-class student. His name is Simon Butcher. You'll love him.' How thoughtlessly one uses that word. 'He's only in his early twenties but he's so marvellously sensible and competent. We make a great team – I wish he could stay. I've never met a student that I've felt more comfortable with, just sitting and talking together. I'll be sorry when his teaching practice is over.'

'Oh?' she said, carelessly.

'The children wouldn't dream of doing anything to upset him, partly because they have some healthy fear – he's a good disciplinarian – and partly because they adore him. He's inexperienced, but already he's a better teacher than I am in some ways.'

'I look forward to meeting him,' she said. But she sounded bored.

'He's very mature for a young college student,' I continued.

'Polly, are you trying to tell me that you've fallen in love with a twenty-year-old youth?'

'No, I'm not,' I snapped. 'He's a friend, almost like a son to me. It's just that most students arrive helpless and at loose ends. This one came along absolutely confident about what he wanted to do. You must surely understand the attraction of that, after all the blank-faced children from college we've had. So that when I get a good one, I'm pleased about it.'
almost like a son to me

85

'Polly, this is the funniest thing I've heard for a long time. I know … we both know … you got your problems, but this is hilarious. Oh my Gawd.'

'For Christ's sake –'

'Of course,' she said, soothingly, but still laughing. 'Just the same, I reserve judgement until I see him tomorrow morning. Who knows? I may fall for him myself. Maybe I'll take one look at him and be carried away.'

I was suddenly uneasy. 'Don't be silly, Maggie,' I said, sharply. 'He's only twenty-three.'

'At it again with your moralising, Polly? Don't worry, I've no interest in little boys. I promise to have affairs only with respectable, middle-aged married men.'

'Sometimes your facetiousness can be tiresome. I simply said he was twenty-three. You don't have to make a big issue out of it. You'll be meeting him in the morning, so I thought it might be nice for you to know a little bit about him first.'

Mag laughed. 'Oh, you do look funny when you get angry, Polly. You seem to forget that I haven't contradicted you once. Though I might ask: what does this paragon look like?'

'I'm sorry, Maggie,' I said, stiffly. 'I happen to think he's a very fine young man and I don't like you making a joke of it. I just say it's unusual to meet someone so thoughtful and mature who's still at college.'

After she left, I was perturbed. Maggie had upset me more deeply than seemed reasonable, but I determined that I would not let it happen again. These good intentions did not last. There is a hiatus in my soul and through that gap she could drive a coach and horses.

86

Mag and I strolled to the school the following morning. The adjoining door was open. Simon Butcher came into her room, held out his hand and said, 'You must be Mrs Miles.'

'Yes,' she said, and they looked at each other carefully.

He took out a knife and began to sharpen his pencil.

'What a beautiful knife,' she said. Ivory and ebony with his initials, S.B.

'Yes, I got it for passing my eleven-plus.'

At that moment, Derek came in and patted Maggie on the arm. 'You're looking gorgeous,' he said.

The whistle went and Simon and I went into our room and began the day's work.

Chapter 4

Although I was looking, I did not see. There's a problem about focal distance in human relationships: in order to observe clearly, you must stand in precisely the right spot. Too close or too far, and the images blur and merge. I was much too near and that's why I did not perceive that she was seducing him.

There were remarks about it, first of all, in the staffroom, just a few witty asides. I paid no attention to them – I was so used to Mag flirting and playing about with male adoration that I regarded it as part of her personality; I was also used to other women making jealous comments. I could not imagine a neutered Maggie. She brought with her a sexual jolt into every room she entered and the feeling of being kicked in the gut by her vibrancy was, by now, so familiar to me that I took it for granted. But Simon came virgin to her peculiar sexual resonance. I don't believe he was literally virgin, but I think he'd never before worshipped and lusted after the same woman at once.

I did notice that he spent a lot of time trying to teach her simple arithmetic – like long division and sums involving mixed fractions, things that even an incompetent primary schoolteacher should be able to do in her sleep. I realise now that she didn't want to learn. I remember her sitting beside him every break, chewing on her little finger and pulling the zipper of her leather boot up and down, up and down. I saw, but I didn't understand.

It was Jane Harmon who finally said it outright. We were alone in the staff-room one dinner hour and I had just poured myself a cup of coffee.

'How's your student?'

'Simon? He's great. Best one I've ever had.'

'Seems to me he isn't completely concentrating on the children. Seems to me he's got a favourite pupil in the next class. I mean, Polly, if you're a teacher, you should save your more – ah – human feelings till after school hours, don't you think? In short, hasn't he enough to do without going gaga over Maggie Miles?'

'Have you ever met a male who didn't go weak at the knees at the sight of her? Don't be idiotic, Jane. All men go gaga over Maggie.'

'Oh I know,' she said bitterly. 'A pair of big blue eyes and Derek's down for the count. He's disgusting. She gets away with murder, all because of those fluttering eyelashes.' She lowered her voice. 'Do you know, I heard from Gillian Loveday – Mark's in Maggie's class – Maggie was giving a lesson on telling the time and she clearly told the children that p.m. was short for post-mortem – she told them she'd looked it up in the abbreviation section at the back of the dictionary because she didn't know. Gillian was livid. I don't know why you're laughing, Polly. I think it's disgraceful.'

'I think it's marvellous. Dear Mag ... I've often felt like death myself by the time afternoon arrives.'

Later, I thought about what had been said, but I had to

believe that Simon was of no special importance to her. I didn't want to venture any further than that. All my life I have tried to close my eyes to the jagged edge of desire.

Finally I mentioned it to Maggie. 'People are talking about you and Simon. You should be more sensible.'

'Why?' she asked coldly. 'Whose business is it?'

I'd expected anger and outrage at the absurdity of linking their names.

'If you react like that, people will think there really is something to gossip about.'

'Well, perhaps there will be,' she said.

I watched them with more understanding after that. Maggie was changed; I had not seen her in love before. Her ivory cheeks became a shade which could be accurately described as Fair Rose No. 7. Soon her father was elevated from a tourist guide into a senator; it seems he had once dabbled in politics, but had certainly never got that far.

'You lied to him,' I said.

'I know. I can't think why. It just came out.'

When she next saw him, she said at once, 'I told you a lie. I'm sorry. My father owned some tourist cabins and he guided people around the lakes – that's all.'

'Why did you say ...' he began, stunned. He was only twenty-three, remember.

'Because I've fallen in love with you,' she said without the slightest hesitation.

The oldest technique in the world, I thought. Except that in Maggie's case there wasn't even the risk of rejection.

'Am I not supposed to say that?' she asked, looking marvellously innocent.

'You bloody fool,' I said, and left the room in furious despair. Of course she'd done it, done it with brazen brilliance. You could always trust Maggie to score her points dramatically. I wondered if that had been why she had so uncharacteristically lied in the first place. I have often noticed that illicit love acts as a strong magnet on a stable life, distorting and wrenching it into new and eccentric patterns.

'But what about Tish?' I asked gently when I saw her later. 'It seems to me you've forgotten all about her.'

She shrugged. 'I think we've been through all this before, theoretically, Polly.'

'Ah yes, but there's something in Goethe, I can't remember it exactly, something about grey theories and golden trees. I think of Tish and Iain – they are your golden trees, the living things, before which theory withers. You can't do it to Tish. You know you can't.'

'I don't know it, Polly. I've always thought obvious propositions need examining. Of course I shall be breaking a promise I made at the age of eighteen. And that's all. This whole business of appealing to duty to your children is one more trick to tie a woman down. It's the weight of a mighty anonymous army coming against you, persecuting you in your sleep when you can't fight back. I refuse to be intimidated. All I stand condemned for is breaking a promise I made fifteen years ago as a totally inexperienced child and let whoever's done no worse than that take up the first stone. Iain and I don't love each other – Simon and I do. There is no rational reason why we shouldn't be happy. Be truthful: a man comes to you and suddenly the sun shines and everything is clear for the first time in your life – the

92

world is golden and the sky is blue and all because of this man. Is it wrong? Is it wrong, Polly Grundy? You'd have everyone clucking their tongues out of envy, they wouldn't do it, oh not they; they haven't had the bloody chance. But Polly, you and he – damn the world. Even if it hasn't happened to you, use your imagination.'

'Stop,' I muttered. 'It's as usual – when one person does it, no, I suppose it doesn't matter. But what if everyone acted as you want to? That's why they pounce upon you – to prevent a general sliding. Most of us simply don't get the kind of chance you're talking about. Of course I don't know the answer. If I were in your shoes I can't guess what I'd say. I hope I'd do the right thing but, truthfully, I don't want the chance presented to me.'

'Liar,' she said at once. 'Everybody wants the chance, just once in a lifetime. Can you think of anything on earth more exhilarating?'

'No, I think it's better that temptation should be in short supply. I haven't got the answer and even if I had, you wouldn't listen. But if you go to bed with Simon, the whole school will know about it within a week.'

'What's it got to do with the school? We won't be doing anything in front of the children.'

'I should hope not. That would be the last straw,' I said, caustically, 'that, combined with your inability to multiply mixed fractions.'

Someone blew the whistle and, like Cinderella, we returned to work.

A few days later, Simon remarked that he had managed

to get on a weekend course for Creative Writing that both Maggie and I had signed up for several weeks earlier.

'I never know how to teach Creative Writing,' Simon said later.

'You think it can be taught?'

'Some of the people at County, the advisers, they can give you little tricks. I think about my teaching all the time, how I can improve it. I try to sort out in my mind how I can give that lesson better next time, how I can organise it so that I can see more children in the same length of time. I've tried to model myself on you, Polly, because I think you're a good teacher.' Irresistible, that. 'I've really tried hard,' he went on. 'It means a lot to me to get a Grade One on my certificate. I'm prepared to work.'

'You'll get there all right. You're the best student I've ever had and I'll be sorry when you go.'

I said this truthfully, but with a pinch of pain. I knew he was heading straight for Maggie's trap and it hurt me to see innocence besmirched.

'So that's why I've applied for the Creative Writing course that you and Maggie are going on in ten days' time.' Ah. It became clear. A residential course. 'I told Mr Lloyd I wanted to go and he phoned through, and there was an empty place.'

'Do you love Maggie?'

He looked uneasy. 'She fascinates me – I can't stop look-ing at her. But she's got a twelve-year-old child. I was brought up very conventionally. I never thought of myself quite like that, with a married woman. I can't get over that, to me, she seems to ... well ... you know, she seems to care for me ... that way. You see, it can't be me, she's so ... I wouldn't want to marry a woman like Maggie. She frightens me. I've known women like her before without being particularly attracted to them, physically. I'm not sure how it'll turn out.'

'I am,' I said, gloomily.

On the day that we were to go on the course, Maggie said, 'I've told Iain.'

'Told Iain what?' But already I felt an ominous tingling.

'Can't you guess? I've told Iain about Simon and me.'

'And ...?'

'And nothing. He wasn't interested.'

'Are you unhinged? He's just a kid of twenty-three.'

'You don't know anything about it.'

'Never mind morality,' I said. 'You're just plain stupid. Concentrate on being in possession of your basic faculties.'

'And where do you get your great experience from, Polly Macdonnell, that experience which helps you lead such a mature and happy life as exemplified by several suicide attempts? Ho, ho, ho. Pots and kettles. All you're saying is what you've heard other people say, stale and old and tired.'

'But what exactly have you told Iain?'

'That we're in love. Don't sneer – I'm telling the truth – I can't do any more than tell the truth. It is true, and I *will* say it, and I won't let your laughter stop me saying it. There's no substitute for experience. I know all about morality: after all, I was raised on the North American prairies where righteousness is rampant. But why do you suppose, over the centuries – poets, they all know there's nothing in heaven or on earth that's stronger than love. And I believe that truth-fulness. There's nothing stronger than that.'

I'd heard Maggie stuck in this banal groove so many times before. Was it worse than my groove? I wondered.

'You mustn't, Maggie.'

By this time, we had reached Simon's car and he was waiting. The absurdity of the situation struck me and I wondered why I had not withdrawn from the course when I knew he would be there. Was I coming as a chaperone?

'Neither of you … you don't know what you're getting into. You think there are no complications. There *will be* complications,' I whispered.

'Drop it, Polly. I've heard your views so often they bore me to death. You babble inanely because you're jealous.'

I almost slapped her. 'Shut up, shut up, shut up …'

'What a wonderful command of the English language you display,' she remarked drily. 'It's on a level with the way you run the rest of your life.'

'I've made a mess of my life,' I said. 'I want to stop you doing the same.'

'You mean you once had a lover and it made you go bananas? Pull the other.'

'Come on, you two,' said Simon.

'No – how can you expect me to go with you on this course – and watch – you – '

'Avert your eyes,' Maggie said.

We got in and travelled in silence for the ten miles it took us to reach our destination. When we got there, we were assigned three rooms in a row off the main hall on the top floor. One person per room. No need to share with a stranger, we were told. They knew, they said, that on courses teachers liked to have a room of their own, a bit of privacy. Maggie and Simon went directly into the first bedroom together without the slightest preamble.

It's in your court now, God, I muttered resentfully to the skies which were cold, leaden and uninterested.

We went down for supper half an hour later. They walked into the dining-room hand in hand.

'Come on, Polly, sit at our table,' Simon said. 'It's going to happen whether you like it or not. There's no need to have a fight about it. We've been such good friends.'

'All right,' I answered. 'Just stop pawing each other, though, can't you?'

'Oh come and sit down,' Maggie said, crossly. 'This is getting ridiculous.' We all wished that I were somewhere else. 'You want us to play Happy Families, but it isn't that way. Dear Clever-clever-Polly. I'm sick of Polly-this and Polly-that, and let's ask Polly, she's so wise. Well, you're not.'

I sat at another table. After supper, we all went to what was called the Conference Room where, in front of a frisky artificial fire, we listened to the guest speaker give a talk on writing poetry. I forgot about Maggie and Simon: all I could think of was poetry and children. I wondered how people got to be experts on anything: by love, or study, or what? I began to think as he talked that although he knew much about poetry, he knew less about children. It's hard to talk about teaching convincingly, because it's something you do, not something you talk about. And quite suddenly I thought: I'm so glad I'm a teacher. It doesn't matter that I'm lacking this esoteric knowledge. I know that isn't the right attitude, but then in teaching you have to balance out wisdom, love and expedience. You've got this quirky, delicate scale which is the mind of a child, and you have to put a little bit on this side and a little bit on that side, so carefully. Always gently because the way of a child is crabwise, weaving back and forth, around and beside, never straightforwardly from A to B. A child's education is always circuitous. I could guess that the speaker had not taught for long before becoming an expert. Still, what he was saying was interesting, even if it was wrong. Simon, who was sitting next to the fire, had dozed off.

The man was talking about 'the child' again. Speakers always think of 'the child' as a twelve- or thirteen-year-old, one who is trembling on the threshold of adolescence. They can remember themselves at that age, you see, so sensitive and intelligent. It's the other bits they can't remember.

After questions were over, it was suggested that we might all like to walk a few hundred yards down the road to the nearest pub 'for some liquid refreshment – ha, ha!' I didn't want to go, but a teacher I'd met at another course a year ago was clinging to me and enthusiastically urging me to have fun, so we set off down the road together. I ignored Maggie and Simon.

At the pub, I found myself wedged into the corner of a small table with the teacher from last year on one side, one of the Big Bosses on the other, and the guest speaker across from us. I ordered a whisky.

'Of course,' our speaker was saying. 'But there's much good poetry that a child can understand and appreciate.

After all, a child's preoccupations are quite different from an adult's.'

'I know,' I said, unsure of how to express what was in my mind. 'I was thinking about the quality,' I continued weakly. 'I've noticed that so much that is passed off as "appropriate" or "childlike" is sheer drivel. You know, every year at the Harvest Festival, the children at our school recite:

> 'Harvest is with us once again
> With apples, plums and pear,
> We'll share with all who are in need,
> To show that we do care.

'And every time I hear that damn verse, I want to scream. I've told my headmaster it's verbal garbage, but he says it's something the child can understand. He says it's the kind of poetry he liked when he was small. Mind you, that I can believe. Try as I will, he won't budge.'

'But what's wrong with giving children poems which are written for them specifically?'

'Because it's often not as good as poetry written for adults. Children belong to the world too – all humanity is one. Poetry written for children is deliberately limited. Generally speaking, you should be reading poems which you have to stretch for and which you can't quite get. Children – no, people – have to learn the same things over and over again, all their lives, each time at a different level. You have to give children the very best you have.'

Why? I wondered. Because it is in homage to ... to ... *timotheos honouring God timothy*

99

'Nobody has ever doubted that. The question is: What is the best?'

'Yes, I know that's the question,' I said, suddenly feeling exhausted and beaten. 'But it hardly matters. I'm in a school where the question of quality is discouraged. Jokey poetry with vocabulary "the child understands" is the in-thing where I teach. It's Jeremy Richards ... he's our chap in charge of English. He's got baby-bright ideas and CLAP CLAP for we're a friend of Jesus and here we come gathering nuts in May ...'

The Big Boss said firmly, 'Jeremy has enthusiasm, drive, intelligence and compassion. It won't be long before he's a Head.'

'I've no doubt of it at all,' I replied. 'Oh, he's no worse than most nowadays. It's just that I stopped, I suppose, about ten years ago. I'm as reactionary as they come. You stand up alone in front of thirty-five children and it's you, alone with your conscience, and them in front of you and there's no point in appealing to experts at that moment. You must do what you know is right. And I'm going to go on doing it. I know I'm giving them nourishment which will grow into muscle. It will one day be what makes their life worth living.'

'You're very arrogant. Have you thought of taking early retirement, Polly?'

I winced. The Big Bosses seem to think when they call you by your first name that it indicates some sort of mateyness. Or maybe they just regard us as Top Juniors.

'Yes, I am very arrogant and no, I haven't thought of taking early retirement.'

100

'Teachers should be humble, recognising that they have much to learn.'

'A convenient theory for Heads and advisers. But there's no point in discussing it,' I said, wearily. 'You see, we're already formed.'

The pub-keeper was calling 'Time!'

'You should go on more courses like this to broaden your mind,' the speaker said.

Ahead of me I could see Maggie and Simon, and I realised that I had forgotten about them for a few hours. Gall and bitterness filled me once more as I heard them laughing. I tripped and involuntarily cursed.

'Shame! Language!' the others teased me.

I went up to my room as soon as we got back to the manor house. I could see them still lingering outside under a tree. Maggie was in the moonlight. Well, that was enough of that. I drew my curtains angrily and then realised, with a shudder, that it was icy cold in the bedroom. The wind shivered through the curtains while, outside, I could hear the cold cry of an owl. I huddled over the radiator, embracing it, and I groaned in my misery at the knowledge of what was to happen. What difference should it make to me? My chest was banging so hard that I wondered if perhaps I were having a heart attack. My God, it was cold. Suddenly I was in a dreadful state, sweating and shivering convulsively, so I went to the sink and ran hot water over my hands in order to steady myself. I heard something against the window and opened the curtain. It was the first snowfall of winter. I didn't look under the tree but twitched the curtain closed again quickly in case they should see me apparently spying.

Then I undressed, but I didn't get into bed because I couldn't lie down. Something was hurting in my chest, in my throat. Since it was snowing, they would have gone in. I looked at the wallpaper – garish, ridiculous roses: I've always loathed roses. Then I turned off the light, climbed under the blankets and began thinking: they are in bed together they are making love together there now go to sleep polly macdonnell and forget it maggie you should not have i did my best iain but she knows her own mind and she chose simon I couldn't sleep, but lay awake, clammy and jittery, through the endless vacuum of that night.

But morning did come and I got up. At breakfast I was grabbed by the clinging teacher from last year's course.

'After we came back last night,' she said, 'I wrote a poem. After all, this is supposed to be a course on Creative Writing.'

'Yes,' I said.

'I worked a long time on it,' she said.

A gloomy foreboding settled over me.

'Would – would – would you like ...?'

'Oh, yes, yes, yes,' I said hastily. 'I'd love to read it.'

Thoughts upon a Weekend at Morley Manor

The dust, the grime, the chalk of seven weeks,
Begins to flake away in this still place,
While each of us a new truth seeks,
A shining honesty, a kind of grace.

The evening falls in quiet peace,
My muscles loosen and relax,

102

I feel my wrinkles all uncrease,
Within these silent cul-de-sacs.

So far from 'Miss, will you correct my work?'
And 'Johnny's fighting on the field!'
And all those petty things that irk,
The wounds of half a term have healed!

Lord, let me use this time apart,
These hallowed hours I, daring, dream,
Rekindle faith, refresh the heart,
And in the ashes find a gleam.

When I return on Monday morn,
To care again for thirty-nine,
I'll bring with me a soul reborn,
Let sweeter patience be the sign.

Well, bugger me, I thought, is this what teachers come to?
    'Do – do you like it?'
    'Were there seven weeks in this last half-term?' I asked, at
a loss for any other kind of comment.
    'Six, but it didn't scan properly. Maybe I could say, "six
whole weeks". That would be more sincere, wouldn't it?'
    'Ah … yes.'
    'I'm thinking of adding another verse about how peaceful
and far from the ordinary world it is – something like "No
Concorde flies above our heads".'
    'But it did,' I replied wickedly, 'yesterday.'

'But not – I mean it in a metaphorical sense. One can be true in one's heart without it being technically true.'

'You mean, as in "But in my heart I've always been faithful to my wife."? Anyhow, have you really got thirty-nine in your class? That's a lot.'

'Forty,' she said, proudly, 'but that didn't scan either and, besides, I couldn't think of anything to rhyme with forty.'

'Sporty, shorty, warty?'

She looked pained. This was apparently not the vocabulary of deep inner peace.

'How long have you been teaching?' I asked suddenly.

'Seventeen years.'

I'd better get out fast, I reflected, before I start drooling on about hallowed hours in silent cul-de-sacs. I was afraid of what the years were doing to me. It was a melancholy thought.

Then we were divided into small groups for discussion and Simon and I found ourselves together. I tried to pretend he wasn't there, but after the session had broken up, he caught me by the arm.

'Come on, Polly. Nothing has changed. We're still friends. After all, it's done now. You don't have to feel any more that you can prevent it.'

'Oh no,' I said, sarcastically. 'How good of you to tell me.'

I started to snivel but I didn't know why. He helped me to a sofa.

'Please tell me why you dragged me into it,' I asked. 'You know I love you both – we're too entangled. Go away, Simon. It's Maggie I want to talk to. We were friends, long before you came. But you came – you came – and everything was spoiled. Both of you have so many gifts. Why aren't you satisfied with what you have?'

'I'm sorry. Polly, I know about … about when you've tried to kill yourself. Mag told me.'

'How kind of her. Oh, here she is. Little Miss Tell-Tale herself.'

'You think … ' Maggie started to say. They made some sort of signal over my head that I didn't quite catch.

'You haven't the faintest idea what I think,' I said bitterly. 'I love anything that is beautiful, is radiant, is full of the joy of life. That's why I love both you and Simon. I'm in love with the glory of the universe and the radiance of the heavens and the beauty of all that glows. In my way, I'm as greedy as you. I want to be part of beauty. I want to be part of your life because of your warmth and your loveliness. I have just as many longings as you have, Maggie.'

They both got up. 'What exactly do you want, Polly? Talk to Simon,' Maggie said, and left.

But I had nothing to say to him.

'You're not being honest,' he said. 'You love one of us but you're setting up a smokescreen because of some truth that you don't want to look at. Don't worry, I won't say any more about it. I know, but I know that you don't want to talk about it.'

'Bugger off. You think it's Maggie.'

'Yes … I don't know what I can say to you that you won't misinterpret.'

'Oh, try me,' I said, harshly. 'We're pinned for an instant at a certain intersection of space and time. We're here, points in eternity, no duration, no magnitude – just here, like Kilroy. Then gone. Why shouldn't you say what you want to say? Why shouldn't I misinterpret it? There is nothing – ' I spoke deliberately ' – that you could say which would shock me. I am prepared for absolutely anything which you wish to say to me.'

'No,' he said. 'I'm not prepared for it. I can't cope with it or with you.'

'You don't want to. Look at me. I am childless, frustrated, on the very edge of my middle age.'

'Stop.'

I did stop. I walked away, wondering why he would not help and then I realised that he had followed me. He sighed.

'You delude yourself, Polly. Sex has to discharge itself some way. It's only because we're here. Like Mount Everest, you know. Lust by itself is transient and embarrassing. Listen, I do know what I'm talking about. I can guess – I'm not blind – you aren't old, Polly.'

'I'm going to make someone very happy one day, you mean? Your kindness is overwhelming. Maybe we could start a card index on possible candidates?'

'Be quiet and listen. You've got your life in one hell of a mess – '

'Oh, that's rich, that is. You're on your final teaching practice and you're having an affair with a married member of staff ten years your senior and you think I – oh, forget it.'

That night I went with the others to the pub again. I drank and drank and drank, out of a longing for all the things I couldn't have.

When we got back to the manor house, I banged on their door. Maggie came at once and pushed me into my own room. She managed to get me mostly undressed, until I was just in my underwear.

'I want to be you, Maggie, radiant. You are the Queen of the whole world and you disperse your glory everywhere. Throw a bit of it my way, Maggie. Don't forsake me. I need part of your love. I need another drink too.'

'Be sensible. Go to bed and forget this silliness. You're terribly drunk and you're saying very stupid things. You've always told me I have my head in the clouds, but what's lurking in your own mind, underneath?'

I tried to speak but she put her hand over my mouth.

'You're saying ridiculous things, Polly dear.'

The room was swimming with despair and desire. 'Maybe, but I still want to say them. I've got to say them!' I cried out. 'I'm human, I need affection, I need love. You don't understand.'

'I understand perfectly. But you've got to get through life, finding love where you can, on the way. You can't over-power people and mug them for it. You're only – what? – forty?'

'I've loved you in a way I've loved no one else,' I said, lurching slightly. 'I didn't want anything from you. I wanted just an exclusive friendship. I'm remarkably undemanding. But I can't bear this business with Simon. I'd do anything for you, Maggie.'

'No. It's not on. The love I feel for Simon, the love I once felt for Iain, even what I felt for Al Farmer and Eddy Culler, that's sex and, most emphatically, that is not what I feel for you, Polly.' She left and closed the door behind her.

'Shorry I meshioned it an merr chrishmash to you too,' I

107

muttered and slumped over. I suppose my strongest feeling was humiliation.

Of course I had to meet Maggie and Simon at breakfast. We sat at the same table and were thoroughly civil. That afternoon, we drove home in silence.

I've often wondered, since that time, if I was … well, you know. I belong to a generation which finds it awkward to formulate thoughts about that subject clearly, let alone talk about it. I don't think so because, like her, I recognise a different quality in relations with men, a sexual thump which has been consistently absent in my dealings with women – except Maggie. Is there perhaps a common wellspring to all our sexuality, and is that wellspring an aboriginal sense of loss?

Chapter 5

The following week, I was at Maggie's house, giving Tish extra spelling lessons – she and Maggie were never on the same wavelength – often you get that between mother and daughter. Besides, Mag's own spelling was hardly a paradigm of excellence.

Tishy had to write a haiku for homework and had got as far as

> Why does the sea surge?
> Who can dry her stinging tears?

which, for a haiku, is like coming to the last chapter of *War and Peace*.

When the doorbell rang, I answered it because I was closest. Now, Simon was school and this was private, so I was surprised to see him at the door. Do you know, I actually thought he'd come to see *me* because he was my student.

'Hello, Simon,' I said. 'Come in. What can I do for you? How did you know I was here?'

Then Maggie came up behind me and he looked over my head at her – and I knew at once that this was the night that they were going to have it out in the open. Why had they chosen a time when she knew that I would be there, or did she hold me in such low esteem that she was unconcerned? I felt trapped and yet I didn't intend to leave. I became aware of a grotesque truth, namely, that I didn't want to be left out.

Iain said, 'You must be Simon.'

Quite suddenly, I wanted to protect poor Iain. So the four of us stood in the small hallway, just like mine, the houses are identical: mirror images. We stumbled through into the sitting-room where Tishy was hunched up over a poetry book on the sofa. She looked up at Simon. Someone should tell her to go to bed, I thought. Now, quickly.

I couldn't move. I just wanted to know what was going to happen next. I knew I ought to leave at once, but I was aching all over with the desire to know what was going to happen.

'Sit down,' Iain said.

I was afraid to look at Maggie because I knew that all my emotions would well up as inappropriate mirth. I was re-minded of a Victorian father wanting to know a suitor's prospects.

'So you're Simon,' Iain continued, and Maggie and Simon and Tish and I all said, 'Yes,' at once.

Then we subsided into silence. Etiquette manuals are not helpful in such circumstances.

Then Maggie said, 'Simon and I are in love.' When a delicate touch was required, she tended to act with consid-erable crassness. I stared at the carpet, scarlet-faced, desperately keeping my eyes away from Tishy. I felt outrage boiling and seething within me as Maggie blithered on about not wanting to hurt anybody.

'I suppose we have to look at all sides of the question,' Iain was saying. That perhaps was the trouble with taking a University of Minnesota Care and Counselling Course.

'Oh, no wonder she prefers Simon,' I said in a fury, but Iain simply carried on.

'We don't own each other, as I've often said. Nonetheless, I think marriage does impose certain duties and obligations.'

I wondered what would happen if I screamed and stood on my head. I glanced at Tishy and saw that her face was a steady surface, unruffled and remote.

'On the one hand, you have a perfectly reasonable desire to lead your own life, a desire in which you know I concur. But you must think of ...' He looked meaningfully at his daughter. We all did. Maggie sighed, but Simon covered his eyes with one hand. She was evidently the dominant partner.

'Maybe if we talk it over, we can decide what's best for all of us,' she said.

'Of course,' agreed Iain.

'You're horrible,' said Tish, looking at her mother. This was the first sensible remark of the evening.

'I want you to understand what we're doing,' Maggie said. 'Your father and I simply live together. It's – one day you'll understand about – '

'Belt up, Mum.'

'You mustn't talk to your mother that way,' Iain said. Maybe clichés are all we have to live by, ultimately. How else to cope with the collision of hearts?

'Why not?'

Simon removed his hand from his eyes and shook his head hopelessly in Tishy's direction.

'We're not trying to hurt you,' he said.

The girl got up, came across the room and kicked him with all her might. He held out his hand, but Tishy glared at him, sat down on the floor at his feet and hid her face in her knees.

'I think,' Maggie continued quietly, 'that nobody needs to get hurt. This is what we have in mind,' she said, taking a swift breath. 'It's that Simon should come here as our lodger. We add to the family, we don't subtract.'

She wasn't much good at arithmetic at the best of times. Iain looked totally staggered.

'What?' he squeaked, and I thought how absurd he sounded in his humiliation. Poor bloody Iain, purple in the face. Tishy began to giggle in a muffled way from her knees. Simon had his face covered once more. Fat lot of use he is, I thought. Then he decided to contribute to the conversation, albeit somewhat haltingly.

'We're in love. We don't – we know – '

'Shut up.' Iain cut him short. 'I've a good mind to punch all your teeth down your stupid baby throat. Get out before I bloody well throw you out.' About time, I thought.

'No,' Maggie said. She stood up.

'No?' Iain asked, and I held myself very still. 'Who says "No" to me in my own house?' I suppose it was not his fault that he had been brought up to expect to be masterful.

'He goes, I go.' Misery and silence hung in the air like cold droplets of fog. Maggie was aware, as she always had been, of her trump card.

'Sit down,' Iain said.

'I – I don't want to cause trouble,' Simon said, and the rest of us, all four of us, simply howled with laughter. Iain's eyes started to stream, but whether it was merriment alone which caused his tears I couldn't say.

'You didn't tell me that your boyfriend was a wit,' he said.

'Dear, dear Simon,' said Maggie, wiping her own eyes. 'Maybe you'd better stay out of this just for the moment.'

Dear, dear Simon was scarlet and Iain knew that he had the upper hand, at least for the moment.

'I should have thought that causing trouble was precisely what you had in mind.'

'No, no,' he writhed. 'I know what it looks like, but – I – I – want it all – all to be all right – for everybody.'

'Very commendable,' Iain replied. 'It does you credit.'

'Truly, I – I don't – ' He looked at Maggie, but she was still tittering hysterically.

'It's like this,' he tried again, his enormous Adam's apple working hard. 'I know – it's wrong – I wasn't brought up to do things like this. I can't defend it – I know it's wrong. It's not that I – I do sort of think it's wrong. I know how you must feel when we say we're in love, but try to understand us. It's – it's passion, that's what it is. It's – more than we – we know what to do about. She loves me, and I love her, but – '

'But you don't want to cause trouble?' Iain suggested helpfully.

'That's it,' said Simon, looking relieved. 'You've hit it on the head. We love each other, but I don't want to break up your family – '

113

'In that case, Simon, I have a suggestion which might provide the best solution for us all.'

'Yes?'

'Fuck off.'

Iain was breathing heavily by now, and sweating too. Tishy had retired to the sofa with a book and appeared to be reading.

'I want to do the right thing,' Simon muttered, lapsing once more into inanity.

'Splendid,' Iain said.

Simon looked at Maggie and whispered, 'What do we do now?' She giggled and I thought, she regards this as a comedy and then I thought, perhaps she's right, sexual passion is one of the great absurdities of life.

Looking at Iain, Simon went on, 'You're really in a better position than I am.'

'It's morally superior,' Iain agreed. 'I think you've diagnosed the situation accurately. You are disrupting a family with your selfishness.'

Tishy stopped pretending to read.

'It's not just me,' Simon finally said in a muffled voice.

Iain nodded genially. I had known him long enough to recognise and be warned by a certain brilliant smile. 'No, of course it's not. Selfishness is very widespread. I wouldn't dream of blaming you alone.'

'He means me,' Maggie murmured superfluously.

'It's society, rotten through and through.' Iain beamed grandly. 'However, I think I've had enough of this joke for one night. Bugger off, Butcher. Go on, I don't want your stinking body in my house a moment longer.'

114

It was true that the lad was unpleasantly odoriferous at the moment, from terror, I imagine. Simon stood up and looked bewildered.

'I don't want you here, little boy.' His voice was like a scouring pad.

'What'll we do?' Simon said to Maggie.

'Shut up, my dear,' she said affectionately. Then she turned to Iain. 'Simon is staying, because I say so,' she said quietly, 'because if he leaves, I go too, and I know you don't want that.'

It must be wonderful to commit all seven deadly sins and know that you will still be loved unconditionally. Perhaps that is the appeal of Christianity.

'I can't live without you, Maggie,' Iain answered just as quietly, and my heart lurched at this wilful exposure of his own nakedness. 'You're not fair. You can't give ultimatums – ultimata, or whatever the bloody hell it is – like that. I know you don't care about Tish, but can't you feel some shame? If anything ever happens to Tishy because of you –'

'For God's sake, don't talk about her as though she weren't here!' Maggie shouted. 'Tish – you know I love you. I won't leave you. But there are certain things – I'm human too. Try to understand. I do care about you.'

'I don't think so,' Tish said with remarkable calm. 'You care about yourself. That's nothing new, is it? You'll do exactly what you want. You always do.'

'You don't understand, love. I've got human feelings, that's all. I want lots of things, but I want you more than anything else. Would you – would you come with us? No …' she said slowly, and I saw that she had assessed Simon's potential accurately. 'But I do love you – you have to believe me.'

'You probably think you do,' Tishy answered. 'But you wouldn't recognise truth if you fell flat on your face over it. You rush into everything; you never think. You've thought you were cute and charming since you were a little girl and you've never grown out of it. It's a game and whatever you do, there's always a big, dramatic scene. How can you say that you love me, but you'll walk out if *he* isn't allowed to stay? What would you do if Dad said, "Go on, go away."?'

'Shush, Tish,' Iain said. He still loved Maggie and wanted her, I marvelled.

'I'm only human,' Maggie burst out angrily again. 'I want my bit of life before I die. It's like sleepwalking, living with you,' she spat out at her husband. 'I have dreams, don't think I'm contented. I've had dreams of a brighter life than you can give me.'

'Dear, dear,' murmured Iain. 'Couldn't you read a better class of novel?'

'Is that all you can say? "Dear, dear," ' she mimicked him. 'Haven't you any feeling, any heart at all? Can't you understand anyone with imagination? Can't you feel the pain of divided feelings?'

Iain said nothing, but his mouth twitched.

'Don't you dare laugh at me!' she shrieked. That is probably the ultimate humiliation for a beautiful and self-centred woman.

'You're acting a damn fool.'

'I am a fool,' she agreed simply. 'I love Simon and he loves me. I'm a new woman because of him. I've been born again, as the God-types say. There's no answer to that. I have to live by love because there isn't any other light to guide me.'

'Try common sense,' suggested Iain.

'If you, Polly, or you, Iain or Tish, if you loved anybody, then you'd understand. I know you hate me and that's because you're jealous. It's because people hate to see other people happy. You know why the stuff about adultery came about – just envy, dog in the manger. I'm not ashamed of what we're doing. We've thought about it very carefully. I'd go to the ends of the earth for Simon. I won't give him up. I don't care what we suffer, or what I have to give up instead. I'd put up with anything for Simon. I'm not afraid of what you can do to me. I'd never be able to face myself in the mirror again if I were a coward.'

'That would certainly free the bathroom for long periods in the morning,' said Iain.

'Maggie,' I said, 'you claim I know nothing about such matters, but I do know the difference between right and wrong. Once you give your word to someone, you've got to keep it. You should have thought about all this before you married Iain – after all, temptation is a pretty universal thing – but now that you have and you've got a child, you should stick with them. You say all sorts of silly things about fulfilling yourself, but there's no way of looking into the future. How can you be so sure of yourself?'

Iain stood up. 'I don't care what you do,' he said. 'Go on, I don't care. Get out, both of you.' But he was not able to mask his love and his longing. His voice cracked and Maggie knew that she had won.

'Sorry,' Maggie said. 'I'm not leaving but I'm not staying

without Simon. I don't want to be forgiven. I know what I want, and single-minded devotion to you isn't it. And you're quite wrong – I do care about Tish, and if you care too, you'll let me stay here with Simon. I beg you,' she said with an apparently vulnerable tremble in her voice.

She was pulling out all the stops. I wonder if she'll get what she wants; she usually does, I reflected.

'There's nothing else I can do but ask to stay here with you and Tish, but with Simon as well. It could only be your pride which would be an impediment – there can't be any other reason. I'm not proud. If we could come to an agreement about this, we could start up a new kind of family, an extended family. It would be good for Tish to live in an atmosphere of truthfulness. Think of it – and you could – think about it – what's good for the goose – '

Iain let out a choking howl and leapt upon her. Simon and I had to pull him back.

'I'll kill you!' he was shouting. At last we pulled him away and he sat down quite suddenly. His face creased and crinkled like a monkey's and, for a few moments, I wondered what had happened. Then I realised that he had started to cry.

'You'll get over it,' Maggie said with a relieved smile. She sighed. 'You'll see that what we've decided is right. We – we can go away – just for tonight – but we'll come back tomorrow. You may find someone too, and we can make a whole new community, an extended family.'

The graduate of the University of Minnesota Care and Counselling Course did not appear to be thinking positive thoughts.

118

'No need to pay a hotel bill,' Iain said harshly. 'I presume you and Romeo wish to sleep together?'

'Yes,' they both said.

There was a long silence during which Tishy looked at them coldly.

'So you've got what you wanted, Mum. "Dear, dear," as Dad would say.'

At least nobody said that she was too young to understand. It seemed to me that she understood perfectly.

'Tish … Tish, dear.'

'It's terribly funny, isn't it?' the girl went on relentlessly. 'A kind of musical chairs.'

'I'd better go,' I said.

I left and went home. I couldn't sleep that night, wondering at the events I'd witnessed. In the twilight of my brain, I thought that I was a judge and that it was up to me to decide on the question of right and wrong, not just in this case, but for every moral dilemma in the history of civilisation. At last I drifted off to sleep, feeling for Iain, but I woke up inexplicably siding with Maggie. There is indeed a worm at the heart of the rose.

Chapter 6

It's my opinion that where Maggie made her mistake was in trying to act in an honest and open fashion by inviting him home, and if there's anything her story proves, it's that you can't domesticate passion. I don't know why they tried – greed, I suppose, wanting to hold everything in their hands at once.

I arrived at school early the next morning after that memorable evening at Maggie's. I was wondering if they'd eloped to the other side of the world and if that would mean that I'd have two classes to look after. My headmaster thinks I am valiant.

Our caretaker came in, holding Bernie Chamberlain up by the collar, almost throttling him. Mr Ford was shaking all over with pious rage.

'Do you know what I heard this young fellow say? Can you guess, Mrs Macdonnell?'

'No, Mr Ford, but I can imagine it must have been very serious to make you so angry,' I obliged, looking sorrowful. Mr Ford's flaps were highly entertaining.

'Tell Mrs Macdonnell,' he hissed, dropping the lad on the floor. 'Tell her *what I heard you say!*'

Bernie looked up at me, squint-eyed.

'Tell Mrs Macdonnell what I heard you say.'

' "Bastard," miss,' the boy quavered expertly.

'Oh, Bernie!' I gasped, trying to convey the impression that the shock was almost too much for my weak heart. 'Never let me hear you say that again.'

'No, miss. I won't never do it again, miss.'

'Won't *ever* do it again, Bernie.'

'No, miss, never.'

After Mr Ford had left, I put the date on the blackboard and shuffled around, preoccupied, tidying and moving things here and there. I couldn't settle to anything definite, being uneasy about what the day would bring. Then a child from a higher class came in.

'Mr Lloyd says can he see you, Mrs Macdonnell?' I sighed and went over to the main building. Had she phoned in ill? Typical of Maggie, typical, typical.

'Ah, Polly. Good to see you. Sit down.' I wondered suddenly if it was not about Maggie – maybe a parent had complained about something. Teachers live in dread of that.

'It's a delicate matter. Maggie's just phoned to say she'll be late. About quarter to ten. She's got a doctor's appointment.'

'Oh, yes?' My resentment was rising once more. Teachers do not have medical appointments in the morning: they wait for the evening surgery. But I doubted if she were anywhere near the doctor's. She was becoming a liar as well as everything else, was she?

'Polly, how is Maggie functioning? She has seemed somewhat distracted lately.'

'Hadn't really noticed,' I said, mechanically.

'Oh, good. Good. I was a bit worried. In some aspects of her work she seems a trifle disorganised.'

'We all have our weak points. I'm not one to judge her.' I suppose that was slimy, sanctimonious and underhanded of me. But I was still very angry. He nodded with understanding.

'Say no more. Can you – please, Polly – look after her class until she comes?'

'Of course, of course. Just what I'd hoped for on a Thursday morning. Think of all the fun with two classes doing practical maths in measurement and volume. I'll bet Mr Ford will be delighted at all the interesting places the sand, water and unit cubes will get to with sixty-five children working on it.'

'Your student can help you.'

'Simon? He's not in either,' I said with bitterness but, of course, Derek Lloyd did not understand.

I'm trying to be honest, to tell you exactly how things were. There's no point in pretending a generosity of spirit which I do not have. And the truth is, I was becoming bitchier by the moment.

'If I'm going to do her work, maybe I should have her salary,' I snapped and left quickly. I decided against slamming the door. There are limits and, besides, it makes one look ridiculous.

In fact, I settled them with easy work and stood malevolently in the common doorway, defying them to make a sound. Not in the least educational, but it's in their interest that I keep my sanity.

They came at last, just past ten, almost at coffee time. Since I was weary and bitter, I said nothing at all but simply made my class get out their times tables books and chant tables. Then they learned their spelling lists. I'm not what you'd call a trendy teacher.

But, whatever I was doing, my heart and stomach and belly were all churning around. I was beginning to see that my emotions were too bound up with Simon and Maggie and Iain and Tish. Why couldn't we go back, say six weeks, before it all started, before we had become entwined in that particular manner? My world seemed to have shrunk unbearably because, by falling in love with each other, they took so much of my own life with them. My soul was withering and I was becoming a ghost before my time. It was the beginning of the waste years. So, all that morning, I kept glancing at Simon, feeling the classroom closing down upon me. The three of us had coffee together in the hut at ten-thirty. We have a little burner for the children to do cooking and we keep a kettle and cups and coffee and sugar and dried milk.

'Are you sure you're feeling well enough to teach?' I asked her sarcastically.

'I'm OK.' A silence.

'I had sixty-five, all by myself this morning,' I blurted out. 'You're unprofessional.'

I should have guessed that this charge was one which she could bear with equanimity. I wished that they would both go away forever.

'I'm sorry, Pol. I'll do the teaching this afternoon and all day tomorrow too,' Simon said. 'It's the least I can do.'

'And I'll take both classes for outdoor games on Monday afternoon,' Maggie said. 'I'm truly sorry and you've been simply wonderful and I don't blame you at all for being furious. It won't happen again.'

I didn't like the way they were being so sweetly reasonable, frustrating my in my desire to hurt.

'Well, what next?' Maggie asked.

'It's the television programme, so both classes will be together anyhow,' I said.

Simon leapt to his feet and told a child who'd poked his head through the door to go and play.

'It's raining, Mr Lloyd says we have to come in.'

Oh, goodie. My favourite: wet break. The children came piling through the door, stamping and shaking themselves like puppies.

She had come perilously close, and I wondered if she knew it. I was certainly unhappy and perhaps that was all that my disapproval amounted to: jealousy. I went into her classroom at twelve o'clock.

'We've got to talk this over,' I said.

'I promise, I won't do it again.'

'I am rather upset,' I admitted, 'but perhaps I'm too bound up with you. I'm trying to think quietly and logically, as an outsider. For some reason I think it's important to me to understand what you're doing.'

'Yes Polly, you are an outsider in the business between Simon and me. That's something you seem to forget. I'm in love with Simon but I can't leave Tish so we've had a sort of compromise. We've talked about things like this for years, Iain and I. About different kinds of marriages. We'd always agreed – in theory – that adultery needn't break up a family. Our marriage – we'd only stayed together for Tish. We each

of us said if anyone else came along we'd try to be accom-
modating. I think it's the best solution, Simon moving in.
Anyhow, it's none of your business.'

I closed my eyes and shook my head painfully. 'You've
left out something. You may have agreed all this in theory
… you're the one always going on about heart and feelings,
but how do you suppose Iain's feeling? You don't consider
that. You start talking about being rational once you've got
your own way. Well, keep thinking about feelings. Iain's.
How would you like to be Iain?'

'He doesn't mind as much as you think. He doesn't – that
part – that part of our marriage – '

'I wouldn't like to be Iain,' I said. 'Would you?'

She didn't answer at first, but finally, after a long pause,
she looked up.

'No,' she said softly. 'But just the same, it's the best of
several undesirable alternatives.'

'But it's wrong,' I said firmly. 'You have to turn back. The
further you go, the worse it will become.'

'Turn back? Simon has come to live with us. It's already
happened – can't you understand that, Polly? It's happened.'

'You should have the decency to admit that what you're
doing is wrong and has been wrong from the first step.'

'Oh, stop bloody lecturing me,' she shouted. 'What's it to
you? What earthly business is it of yours? You lead a
cramped little miserable life, so you're trying to live vicariously through me, is that it?' Bull's-eye, Maggie.

Bernie catapulted himself through the door, beaming.

'Raining! Indoor lunch break too.'

'So it's got nothing to do with you, do you understand?'
She shrugged angrily and then began again. 'After all, we're
doing it for Tish. I want to show her what two people in love
are like instead of just holding up a sterile marriage to copy,
making her think that's all love is – sharing a house and a
bank account. Look what he gave me,' she added after a
moment, and there was Simon's mother-of-pearl pen-knife.

'Mrs Miles, where's the computer paper?'

'In the box by the window, Jessica. We exchanged gifts,'
she continued. 'I gave him my painting of the purple Madonna.'

'Why – I mean – if he's living with you – it can't matter
much who owns it.' Unless he leaves, I thought.

'Some day we'll be able to live on our own and then –
Peter, leave Jenny alone – it's just that we wanted to give
each other something that was precious to us – sort of
symbolic, you know.' She ran her forefinger over the pen-
knife and I noticed again the ebony initials, S.B.

Morality is terribly confused ground. It was better to live
by the rules, I thought. What would you do if you had to
submit every act to long and painful analysis? And risk
every single one of your actions upon a wrong way of
looking at the world? I hate uncertainty. It unhinges me. I
found my mind freezing into paralysis.

'Mrs Macdonnell, Fiona says I stink.'

You do. Have a bath when you go home.

'Just ignore her, dear.'

The lunch break was over and it was time for the afternoon session. Simon was taking a music lesson right after
the register so I didn't have much to do except sit and watch

him. He had a guitar – all students seem to have them these days – and he strummed and taught them an uninspiring tune about a teddy bear. I become impatient with this one, two, three, Teddy's up the tree drivel which is said to be appropriate and childlike. As if he had nothing else to choose from. So I sat and glared and the children sang it and loved it. Then quiet reading for half an hour, the most valuable time of the day. Before I hear the slow readers, I take my copy of *The Times* and turn it upside down. I struggle with the sound and the sense in the first leader for a few moments to give myself patience and understanding when I listen to Mark Armstrong hurling himself miserably at the shapes in the Happy Reading series. I always do a bit of upside-down reading before I take the slow ones, but never for very long because I don't want to get good at it. And the whole time, I was aching with my hurt. I'm not living my own life, I told myself. This is waste time.

It was still raining by afternoon break, so we left the duty teacher to supervise Indoor Fights and went to the main building for coffee. In the staff-room, people seemed to have guessed what had happened. We were almost hit by the excitement as we walked through the door.

'You'll soon be finished your time here?' one of the teachers suggested meaningfully to Simon.

'Yes ...'

'Have you got a job to go to? I suppose you'll be off somewhere like London then?'

'No, I want to stay in the area.' He looked towards Maggie for support.

'That's not very wise, you know. There are no jobs going around here.'

Simon looked at the floor and Maggie sat still and trembling, her lips in a hard line. I held myself tense and steady, wondering who would say something catastrophic.

'You haven't got a family around here, have you?' Jane Harmon persisted.

'In a manner of speaking, yes, I have,' he replied.

'A brother or sister?'

Maggie sat without moving, the fire building up within her.

'No, it's not a brother or a sister,' she said.

Derek Lloyd came in and looked oddly at them and they returned his private glance. I surmised that Maggie had told him.

'All sorted out now?' he asked, cheerfully.

'More or less,' Maggie said.

'Yes, yes,' Simon burbled. And then quietly to him, 'Thank you.'

'We've just been telling Simon he ought to move away if he wants to get a job.' Someone in the corner giggled and Simon got up and left. Chicken-livered.

'Well, that's certainly true,' Derek agreed ponderously, looking at the door. 'Though – ha, ha – he might have personal reasons for staying, eh, Mrs Miles?'

'*Cherchez la femme!*'

'What on earth do you mean?' Maggie asked coolly. She had gone white. 'I don't like you to talk like that,' she said in her clear American voice and there was a hush. 'As must be perfectly obvious to you all, Simon and I are in love with each other – '

'Never!'

I turned on Jane Harmon, enraged. 'Stop it,' I spluttered. That stunned everybody.

'What's wrong, Polly? Why do you care?' Jane said in her small, chilly voice. I thought to myself: Maggie and I are friends.

'Simon has moved in with Iain and me,' Maggie said. 'And Tish,' she added with an obvious effort a moment later. She was pitifully vulnerable.

'What does Iain think?' Jane asked. Don't answer, I thought furiously. She doesn't really want to know. She'll save up your answer to play back later like a tape-recording to everyone who isn't here now. She was wearing her Sunday best face, caring, concerned and compassionate.

'He doesn't regard me as a possession,' Maggie was saying. She sounded affected and ridiculous. 'We think that everybody belongs only to themselves.'

'Well, that's fascinating,' someone else said. 'But how about the children?'

'Nobody owns anybody else, not parents, not children. You have only one duty in life and that is to yourself – and to others, of course, not to hurt them.'

'While fulfilling your duty to yourself, what if it conflicts with another person's duty to himself?' Little daggers finding their marks.

'I don't believe it ever really does,' Maggie answered fatuously. 'Not really. Not deep down. If you just follow your heart, things will eventually come out right. If you're truthful.'

'Oh, don't be so silly,' I snapped. I had forgotten that they were all against her and that I was supposed to be her friend. 'You go in like a hippopotamus trampling on everybody and hooting "I love Simon." Ask anybody who's ever known you – you know you were reasonably happy until Simon came along. You can't pretend you were imprisoned in a castle tower. You laughed and enjoyed yourself and had fun. And if Simon went away – well, of course it would hurt, but you'd get over it. We've all had those kind of feelings. You can be damn sure that any married woman by the time she's forty has been in love with someone else.' I stopped dead because it had just occurred to me, for the first time ever, to wonder if John had been in love with another woman at any time during our marriage. It was such an astonishing supposition that I sat there with my mouth open. In the silence, I remembered we were not alone and I blushed scarlet. 'I'm sorry,' I muttered.

'But sometimes marriages do break down,' Jane said maliciously. 'Sometimes there's a point of no return. Or so I've heard,' she added hastily, afraid that her own marriage might be open to speculation. 'Tell us more, Maggie.'

But I sat, silent and stunned, not listening to her reply, thinking about John and his humanity. Later, when I got back to the classroom, I lit into Simon.

'Couldn't you have stayed and supported her, or were you afraid it would go against you on your record?' I demanded and then, without giving him time to reply, I added bitterly, 'Typical of Maggie. Break's over and she's not back

131

yet. I see I'll have two classes to look after again while she's still stretched out in the staff-room.'

'Don't you know that break is only fifteen minutes?' I said shortly when she came dashing in. 'Come on,' I turned to Simon. 'Let's get on with the teaching.' Most of my anger was jealousy, envy, hurt feelings, but part of it sprang from something else: outrage that orthodoxy and order were being openly flouted. I am a timid and conventional woman.

That evening Tish came over to see me. 'There's nothing at all you can do,' I said bluntly. 'You're thirteen, you ought to start thinking for yourself. Oh, don't blubber,' I added sharply. You must think I'm callous but, truly, I was thinking of Tish in the long run. 'At least one of you has to act responsibly. I don't feel the least bit sorry for you, Tish. Another five or six years, you'll have a life of our own, free from all this ridiculous mess. Until then, try to act in a halfway grown-up fashion. If your parents are utter fools, it's up to you to try not to be. You've only got one life: use it thoughtfully. Look at everything with clear and steady eyes and then decide what you're going to do. You have to accept that what you're faced with is a regrettable *fait accompli*. Ignore the fact that she's your mother. In the long run, it's yourself you have to live with. So harden yourself, grow up.'

But she just stared at me coldly. 'Why are you getting so excited, Mrs Macdonnell?' she said. 'I didn't ask for your advice.'

I have always been impelled, all my life, to tell other people what to do, to give my little bit of good advice. I

132

found myself loving Maggie and hating her, attacking and defending. Everybody spoke about the affair in the staff-room and there I did try to defend her. She needed me in that staff-room. They walked to school each day, hand in hand, defying people to look. By this time, I felt drained and grey.

She kept reiterating that she was not ashamed. 'Iain accepts everything – I can't be expected to give over my entire life to Tishy. Why should anyone give over their entire life to another person? Everybody's equally valuable. I don't know if I'm doing right or wrong,' she broke down, suddenly sobbing. 'I only know – I know – it's the only thing I can do. I haven't got a choice. All I know is that I was so desperately unhappy before. You said I wasn't, that I laughed. You don't know about it. Am I supposed to go back to that, lifeless and unhappy, sitting watching the world go by, the days drifting by? Why should I wait, giving up my years to this grey prison? Do you think I should abandon Tish, is that it? That's so much tidier, isn't it? – that I should run away with Simon, that Iain should be seen to be a martyr – well, it hadn't been like that, not one little bit and it's not going to be that way.'

I said, 'I can certainly see why you don't want to leave – Simon won't make enough money for years to keep you in the style to which you've become accustomed, will he?' That was nasty, I know, and she gasped. 'As it is, there's a certain question of professional ethics. There might be – I've heard rumours – people are wanting you to go very much. It's acutely embarrassing working beside you.' I'd hurt her badly this time.

The children came rushing in as the whistle blew and

133

Maggie went into her room, banging the door viciously behind her. Unfortunately, she caught her skirt in it and had to go through the scene a second time. I went over and yanked it open.

'Mr Butcher!' I called in a peremptory tone. 'I believe you're in here with me? I wish you'd remember you're still on teaching practice,' I added between my teeth.

He began telling them about the Fire of London. He did it well. He was a good teacher, I had to admit it. By the end of the afternoon, I was too tired to be angry.

When the last child had gone he said, 'I want to tell you that it's going to work out all right. We've talked, all of us, and we've come to quite a reasonable agreement. I'm staying and Iain – there's a woman – you see, it isn't just Maggie.'

'I don't believe you. If he says that, it's just to try to salvage some dignity. It can't be true. Iain isn't like that, not like that at all.' I was remembering so many things, seven years back. 'You and Maggie think it will sound better for you, so you're putting it about.' I would not believe it. I would not believe it. I would not believe it.

'But it's true. Iain has his share of ordinary feelings. There's a girl where he works. You see, things are not as simple as you would have them, Polly, dear. You felt that he was morally superior – now that's true, isn't it? You could keep saying "Poor Iain" over and over again – you don't like to admit that you have no reason to condemn us any more. I didn't want to tell you, neither did Maggie. We wanted to persuade you on what we thought was the only important issue – freedom. And we stick by that: even if Iain were still the perfect husband you think he is, we'd be doing the right

134

thing all the same. Now please – we do care what you think, though God knows why. I'm going now. Think about what I've said.'

I sat quite still for about forty-five minutes, hardly able to breathe for the consternation that I felt. Then I walked down to the river and sat for a long, long time watching the swans preening themselves. Every bone of my body and every beat of my heart was misery to me. I couldn't move; I simply sat watching with the tears rolling down my face. I had believed so completely, first in Iain and then in Simon, and in both cases I had been made a fool of. It has happened over and over again, all my life, from my earliest years, a long chronicle of trust betrayed. And ten righteous men were not found at Sodom. My mind has been constructed so that I have to analyse, I must understand things and, when I've understood them, then I must pass judgement. At that point I thought, no, it's too much, and I got up. The river was there and I felt again the old urge, convulsive and bizarre as ever. But no one was around which gave me less than a sporting chance of survival. I went back to the school and did my marking.

Christmas was not as awkward as it might have been. John and I went up to Aberdeen to be with his parents and I forgot about Maggie and Iain and Tish and Simon as I put up streamers and sang hymns and agreed that Christmas was really for children.

> Cold on his cradle the dewdrops are shining,
> Low lies his head with the beasts of the stall;
> *angels adore tim in slumber reclining,*
> *infant so innocent i have lost all*

135

Then, of course, when we went back for the new term, Simon's teaching practice had ended. I used to see him set out early for his final six months at college. I wrote a good report on him for his record because there was nothing else I could truthfully do. As for what he had told me, I had not yet seen evidence of any woman in Iain's life. When I mentioned it to Maggie, she shrugged indifferently and turned the conversation to Simon.

'He'll have to get a job when he finishes his course.'

'Not in Oxfordshire,' I observed.

'Then perhaps he'll do something other than teach,' she replied sharply. 'Teaching's not so wonderful. And it doesn't pay all that well either,' she added.

Meanwhile Tishy was growing up, quite marvellously. I thought: others have survived and she will too. We went for a hike in the woods one day, early in the New Year, and I perceived that she had undergone a transformation similar to my own – a draining of emotion. She told me about her painting and how it helped her put her world in order.

'What are you going to do with yourself later?' I asked her. 'How about your painting? Is it really important to you?'

'Yes,' she said seriously. 'I'm beginning to understand that kind of feeling that painting is more important than anything – to think that it might be worth giving up everything else, just to paint. I want to make sense of things. I can almost understand about Mum now, but that doesn't excuse her, does it? I forgive her but there is something to forgive. Really to forgive. I'm never going to do that sort of thing to my children.'

'Wait a few more years,' I said. 'It's rash to tempt the gods that way.'

It became noticeable as time went on that Simon had been right about Iain. The only thing for which I had not been prepared was the eclecticism of his taste. He had a rapid and varied turnover. Yes, I know I sound bitter. I had loved him once, even though he had withdrawn from me, but I'd somehow convinced myself that it was I who had rejected him. I had thought of him as a dear, flawed, injured hero and how there had been something gallant about the way he had accepted Simon into the household. It hadn't occurred to me for a moment that it was simply part of a bargain that he'd struck with Maggie. When Mag did it, openly, everyone scorned and reviled her. But when Iain did the same, only more, people said, 'Poor man. You can hardly blame him.'

So life lurched on next door and we all agreed that the convolutions were Maggie's fault. But times do change and what seemed shocking then seems less so today. I have to say that, after a time, everyone in that peculiar household seemed to get on well, laughing and joking and being pleasant to one another. I sometimes used to wish I could join ... there, I've said it. I felt such envy of their obvious ease and freedom, nobody apparently upset by anybody's conduct. Yet I knew, in the very deepest section of my soul, that I could never be happy living like that. It came to me one day when I was in Mag's house and needed the loo. It wasn't until I'd finished that I realised, with shock, that I'd instinctively hovered above it as though it were a public toilet. I have a streak of sexual guilt that runs straight through me and I could never be happy without following the agreed rules. I would live from terror to terror, always wondering when the gods would swoop. And, considering what happened later, I would be right to be anxious.

Chapter 7

I don't remember much about my own adolescence – just a sense of physical absurdity, that my body was gathering flesh beyond my control. It was similar to what I later came to experience in pregnancy, a time of transition with only the word of others that you would emerge as a swan. That's all I can remember of being thirteen and fourteen, though I do have one photograph of myself, shoulders raised and fists clenched, staring miserably down at the two sprouting embarrassments at the front of my chest.

I thought of that the other day when I came across this picture of Tish when she was thirteen. She had a rotten time, partly because her mother, who should have been diluting her own sexuality, was beginning to throb with carnal awareness. This was bewildering because just then the child needed a stretch of dullness and stability.

In her secondary school she claimed, as usual, that the teachers were 'picking on me' – but then Tish had always felt this since her earliest days in the infant school. I realise now that she was more like Maggie than I imagined in that she needed uncritical support. She had a debased opinion of herself which she assumed that others shared.

She was pretty hopeless in all subjects except art and she was too timid to do anything but cringe at sarcasm. She used to slide down in her seat behind her desk in the back row and hope that she would become invisible. I presume she succeeded. You'd have to be superhuman to devote a great deal of time to a child who makes no claims on your attention. She wore layer upon layer of blouses and pullovers under her blazer to camouflage the front of her. Along with what she was growing under all the sweaters, she was also developing a bad posture and a worried look. Whenever I saw her, she appeared flushed, untidy and sweaty. Maggie told me that Tish had started her periods and was pleased about it and I wondered how Maggie knew that. I expect she said something like, 'You must be very pleased to be so grown-up,' whereupon the child had probably muttered, 'Yeah' between her teeth, for I had not noticed that Tish was markedly more forthcoming with her own parents than she was with me.

Tayfields Comprehensive, which was on the outskirts of Oxford, was huge compared to Breckling (C of E) which had a roll of only 176 pupils. Tayfields was bound to be intimidating because of its size. I once went there on a cold February day when, through some misfortune, the heating had broken down. Everywhere our group went, workmen were banging about, trying to find the cause of the problem. In one or two places, they'd taken the floor boards up and we had to edge past gaping, evil-smelling holes. At break-time, we went to the staff-room and watched a herd of teachers rush through the door to fall speechlessly into nearby chairs where they remained, shell-shocked and immobile, until fifteen minutes later another bell wrenched them from their seats and sent them stumbling back into the classrooms. To me – I, who have, over the years, rejoiced in teaching with my whole heart – the scene was unspeakably depressing. I went out into the main corridor where a cold wind blew from one unheated end to the other and shrill groups of fourteen-year-olds pushed their way through another class surging in the opposite direction, lungs and elbows both working to maximum capacity. Then I remembered something that Simone Weil once said – that what humanity needed was silence and warmth, but what it got was icy pandemonium. And Tayfields was the icy pandemonium to which Tishy Miles had been assigned.

I sometimes used to lie awake at night, wondering if there was anything I could do, wondering if already the course of Tishy's life had been decided. Have you ever been awake in the middle of the night when your heart is still with cold fear, when all whom you love are stalked by danger and you lie there, twisting yourself about, wanting to warn and protect, when every car door slammed for miles about is someone coming to announce the death of one you love? You lie rigid, feeling it is tempting the gods to even think of sleep, knowing that if you endure the horror of waiting in the black silence, why, a worse horror may be averted. Not that you'd presume to strike a bargain like that with the gods. They would be certain to punish you for making yourself equal. You can only lie there and hope that being prepared for the worst will somehow count in your favour, somewhere. There have been no untroubled hearts since Eden closed behind us.

Tishy stole five pounds from a teacher's desk in the third year and was found out. She was seen putting it into her own wallet. Of course, as soon as she was caught, she was in torrents of tears, begging that her parents should not be told. But, naturally, the school informed Iain and Maggie, who promptly began agonising over whether their own actions had led to stress for Tish, finally deciding that the whole web was 'too complex for easy answers'. Situations become morally ambiguous only when you decide to do something which you know is wrong, which is why they fussed and talked about the grey areas of responsibility. The saddest part was that they believed their contortions. Once you miss your way the fog closes in.

Tishy Miles very gradually developed into a pert and cheeky girl, able to return an insolent reply. Poor child. She lost her invisibility and was endlessly in trouble for fooling about in class, for not doing her homework, for rudeness to a teacher. She muttered that she would leave school forever the day she had her sixteenth birthday. I told her not to be absurd, that the glories of education were for all people and that she would regret it if she hurled herself out at the first opportunity. Hollow, hollow.

She just smiled at me, and said, 'You've been a teacher for too long, Mrs Macdonnell. You think everybody's troubles can be cured by more years at school. How does a know-ledge of the French subjunctive help me to know what I should do with my life?' Her laughter was full of scorn.

'Everything you learn gives your life a little more rich-ness, gives you a few more hooks to hang your experiences on,' I said, gently.

She looked ghastly during her adolescence. She'd always been skinny in primary school, but now she put on weight rapidly and became thick and lumpish. She also came out in

142

aggressive spots and no amount of creams and lotions would make them go. She never got any better at her academic studies: she scrabbled along at the bottom of whichever class she was in at any given time. At Tayfields they were concerned to show that comprehensive education 'worked' and so they concentrated on their bright stream. She drifted resentfully from class to class, confirmed only in the sense of her own failure. I realise now that she had no friends.

Surely someone should have done something about it long before she was fourteen? Because, of course, it had all begun years ago, back in the primary school when we desperately used to mutter, 'It's only a phase' or 'She'll soon be over the hump' or 'She seems better this year.' Because, of course, except for her time with Phil Sparling, she never did get better. She never was happy. I know that now. *is my son happy?* She tried to tell us for years, and we closed our eyes because there was nothing we could do and we were afraid to try and then fail. Resentfully, we felt that it must be Tishy's own fault.

She was, as the saying goes, a lost soul, seldom smiling. I remember a conversation we had on a bus about six months after Simon had settled in.

'He's going to do supply teaching in Oxford when he finishes,' she said bitterly.

'It's better than nothing,' I said, hating my schoolmistress voice. It's a curse to put on the cap of a profession and then find that you can't tear it off, even when it's inappropriate.

'So you think it's good?' she asked me. I didn't reply and she giggled. 'I don't think you notice what you say,' she went on. 'Schoolteachers and parents and vicars – you always know what they're going to say before they open their mouths. You're all so predictable. You learned about twenty years ago what answer to make to any remark.'

'Too true, Tish,' I said without thinking.

'There you go again. You might see what I mean if you thought about it.'

'Yes,' I said, 'honest, I really do see what you mean.' We rode the rest of the way into Oxford in comfortable and friendly silence.

'Come and have coffee with me,' I said as we got off the bus, and we found a delightful place, high up, where we could look down on the passers-by in Cornmarket.

'I keep wondering what I want to do when I leave school,' she said. 'I'm not good enough to be a painter. I want to be something useful,' she burst out. 'Not like my mother, always out to see what she can get for herself. I want to be fair and not grab for myself. There's Mum teaching little children all day long and look at the way she acts. She shouldn't be a teacher.'

We do not forgive our parents until we have children of our own, I thought, and then in anguish wondered if my sterility meant that my soul could grow no further.

'You'd make teachers hold a Diploma in Morality as well as Education?'

'Yes, I would, don't laugh,' she said, flushing. 'I don't see how you can be one thing in your private life and another thing for the outside world. I think she ought to think about other people before she thinks about herself.'

'The Brownie-Guide promise?' I said, smiling. Tishy

144

glowered and looked sulky. After a moment, she paid for her own coffee and left.

I ordered another cup and wondered if Maggie's actions were being condemned because they were so jarring. Not many wives bring their lovers home, not just for tea but for bed and breakfast. I told myself that you cannot condemn a person just because you find them upsetting. After all, Christ jarred, Socrates jarred, Galileo jarred, the Maid of Orleans jarred. But they were geniuses. Maggie was a weak and pretty woman whose innovative actions were entered into for completely selfish reasons. I wonder that Iain and Maggie didn't simply get a divorce and then Maggie could have married Simon – it might have saved so much tangle.

I thought for a long time afterwards about Tishy and her struggles. She had the most dreadful nightmares all her life and once Simon came to live and share Maggie's bed, the child was discouraged from calling out to her mother in the middle of the night. So she suffered alone.

I haven't told you much about Simon because he was the intruder, so to speak. Yet I have every reason to believe that before he met Maggie, Simon Butcher was a blameless lad of decent upbringing and high idealism. She corrupted him – she ruined him totally for the rest of his life. I keep remembering the first time that Derek Lloyd brought him through my classroom door and introduced him as my student, how eager he looked. Oh yes, while he was at our school he certainly worked – making wallcharts, mounting displays, spending hours reading and marking the children's work. He was a dedicated teacher. Often he didn't even bother with coffee breaks, he was so busy preparing the next lesson. Or at least until he met Maggie. But then he became infatuated almost at once, and at once he felt guilt and anxiety. But, of course, when she showed him that his passion was not one-sided, he forgot his guilt in joy. He felt as we all do when we are in love, that he could do no wrong, that the world was his and, of course, his happiness was infectious and spread to the children. During that first dizzy period, he did phenomenally well in the classroom because one's teaching always improves when one is emotionally raw-edged. I watched them both with envy; perhaps, I told myself, perhaps one day the same kind of sexual miracle will happen for me. Fairy stories.

I've always tried to be a good and conscientious teacher, but something like that, in your own classroom, throws you a bit. I'd go home every evening, worried and on edge, because I was afraid the children would notice something.

'You fuss too much, Pol,' Simon used to say to me gently.

'That does tend to be a characteristic of mine,' I answered.

Over and over, round in circles. That's what it did to me, chained me to a wheel of cause and effect so that I could never be free. That's what Margaret Miles did to us all, to me and to Iain and to Simon and, above all – to Tish.

Chapter 8

My days go on: I keep teaching. But now – these days – I have less of value to tell people, though I am still aware that the heart of all teaching is to direct the minds of the young to the best – only, always, the best. Keep always the best, the best in front of their eyes and then one day they will recognise the second-rate for what it is. 'And if yer a friend of Jeezuz CLAP TRAP CLAP then yer a friend of mine' indeed.

But I was telling you about Tish as I remember her at fourteen with her really terrifying displays, raging, ranting, hurling books upon the floor. Almost spitting at Simon and Mag and Iain. Maggie said that she grew to dread the time that Tish arrived home from school and lurched into the kitchen. She took to having a shot of gin in preparation.

'We don't do anything right in her eyes. You can't have a civil word with her but she throws it back at you.'

I knew what she meant. I'd heard Tish sometimes when the windows were open. Love is unreasonable. When Tish was fourteen, she was totally unlovable but we kept loving her. With that age, you don't get much return from devotion. She was supercilious and dissected us all without pity. It can be devastating to hear yourself described by a cold-hearted child. We tried to laugh. Once I retaliated and made a light jest about Tishy's pimples and I remember how she broke into tormented sobs. Yes, I remember. I remember it in the middle of the night. She was so unhappy, so solitary. I think again of the misery of adolescence, or at least what I have read of it for, as I have said, that time is a blank in my own life. I remember listening, late at night, to Prokofiev – I remember the one word which recurred again and again in my diary was 'despair'. That's all. But Tish's blotchy face used to stir up, not exactly memories of my own adolescence, but terror of the memories. I disassociated myself from Tish and her distress because I could not bear to be pushed back in time. I could not enter imaginatively into her inward turmoil because once is enough. Once is enough.

There was an awesome accuracy to her insults. All my life I've been aware of being two-faced but I thought I had kept the fact well hidden. I tell myself that it's because of my broad sympathies that I can see so many sides to a question. But that isn't true. I'm not an impassive canvas upon which many minds may paint. I'm a cowardly chameleon, always taking the easiest way out, always sympathising with the view that will get me into the least trouble at that particular moment. I lie awake just before dawn, and I know that I am contemptible. Tishy seemed to know all this too. The past leaps up, and up again, to gnaw at me. *i have been punished enough, i have been punished enough.*

Now for Tish, as for other children of that age, no help was forthcoming. The terror of those years is unimaginable. That is why I could not be a secondary schoolteacher. I would refuse to try to imagine it, and I would be harsh and without understanding. Some things are too painful to be experienced vicariously, and that is why the victims are cut off from the rest of us.

I remember so many things about Tish, especially in primary school, before she turned unpleasant – laughter, telling me about King Harold and the poor lady called Edith. Now I watched her, day by day, slouching down the road on her way to catch the school bus to Tayfields.

We felt with some concern – Maggie, Simon, Iain and myself – and even John remarked upon it wryly – we felt, when she was fourteen, that she had chosen unsuitable companions. I say 'companions' because I don't think Tish had a friend, not the sort of friend before whom you can uncover your heart. But the group of girls that Tishy strutted about with seemed to us as unpleasant as herself, and no doubt the parents of the other girls viewed Tish with distaste also. The gang was noisy and clumping, elbowing people out of its way on the street. Yet whenever she saw me, she immediately looked embarrassed, smiled, and lowered her eyes. For all the slogans painted across her jacket, she was scarcely more than a little girl. Such a small step backwards to the baby gurgling in her cot by the Chianti lamp.

I think the worst row came when she shaved her head, preparatory, I believe, to dyeing the bristles a fetching combination of lime green and haemorrhage red. It did not get to that stage, of course, for Iain intervened decisively and explosively. I think if it had been left to Maggie, she would simply have wrung her hands. You may wonder why they did not take a firm stand earlier, but it's difficult to lecture your child on observing the social conventions if you are

149

flouting them yourself. They all were aware of this, and it gave Tishy the upper hand for long periods at a time.

Maggie, meanwhile, had read plenty of articles in the liberal press on how the fourteen-year-old of today had a full-scale throbbing sex life, so she took Tish aside and offered her contraceptive advice. The child looked at her mother with such contempt and horror that Maggie backed off and never mentioned the subject again. Two ships passing in the night.

I'll tell you about a time which I cannot forget. Whenever I sit in this kitchen, I'm reminded. I was on my own, John as usual working half the night at the hospital. I'd been reading and thinking, not able to sleep, walking back and forth in the sitting-room, hair in curlers, and I'd just decided I'd better go to bed because it was past one in the morning, when there was a banging on the door. I hate that when I'm alone at night because, being a doctor's house, you've got to answer. You can't ignore it, even though it's usually just a drunk having fun. But as soon as I got into the hall, I could see through the glass part of the door that it was the police. There's something harrowing about those fluorescent white stripes against the darkness of night. I opened the door and there they were, both horribly large and real. One had red hair and a beard and the other one had very crooked teeth.

'Does Isabella Miles live here?' one of them asked.

I don't know why I said 'Yes.' But I did, and then added, 'Why do you want to know? What has she done?'

'We've got a very sick little girl here in the van. She's in pretty bad condition,' said one of the policemen.

150

Raped, beaten up, in a car accident ...? They got her out of the Black Maria and almost carried her into the house.

'Bring her into the kitchen.'

They dropped her into a chair, the same chair she'd sat and sobbed in four years earlier on the day I'd asked her how she was getting on at school. I sat down quickly on another chair and retched.

'What's wrong with her?' I asked, though it was obvious. They ignored my question.

'How old is she?'

'Fifteen yesterday.'

'Now that's under-age for drinking. Really under-age, you know.'

'Who gave it to her?' I asked angrily. 'It's an offence to supply alcohol to a minor.'

The older officer shrugged. Tish's face was smeared with dirt and her new velveteen jacket was torn. There was a bruise over one eye. Her hair stood up in pathetic tufts, like the hair on the comic strip character who's just seen a ghost. I began to cry and then realised that I would have to phone next door.

'Where did you find her?'

'We had a 999 call. A man walking his dog found her lying unconscious in the middle of Bassett Road.'

Cars – unconscious – Bassett Road – lying unconscious – cars – lorries – lying unconscious on Bassett Road – cars – wheels – blood. My dear Tish. I began to sob hysterically.

'She's not my child,' I choked. 'We'll have to get her mother.'

He got out his notebook for an address.

151

'No, it's just next door, she lives next door, I lied, she's not my child, she has nothing to do with me.'

'What?'

'I know – know – I am – drunk. I'm quite aware.' Tish was carefully slurring her words.

'Yes, you are,' I agreed.

'Lady, are you all right?' asked the red-bearded policeman.

'No, man, I'm on the verge of a mental breakdown,' I said sweetly.

'She goes – bananas – sometimes.'

'Thank you, Tish. Very helpful.'

The policeman with crooked teeth sighed. 'Do you know where this young lady lives?'

'I live here. She's my mother,' said Tish.

'I'm not your mother. I'm not even a relation. I'm nothing to do with you at all. I'll phone your mother.'

'I am Isabella Macdonnell and I live at 9 Rutherford Drive.'

As the policeman wrote it down, I wondered where on earth she had got that address. I phoned Maggie and it was answered immediately by Simon who had seen the police van, but not its occupant. They came at once.

'Iain's away for a few days,' Maggie said shortly. I wondered with some bitterness about the circumstances of his trip, but then Mag and Simon went into the kitchen and pulled up chairs beside Tish.

'Could I have your names, please? Are you her parents?'

'Yes,' said Maggie.

'No,' said Simon.

'I don't know you. Who are you?' said Tish.

Maggie looked at me in panic and I shrugged.

'Who am I?' I said to Tishy.

'You are my mother.'

The police, after a few more questions, decided to leave. The bearded one spoke quietly to Maggie, but I overheard.

'I'd be careful about your neighbour here. She doesn't seem quite right.'

'She's totally unbalanced,' Maggie replied carelessly, 'but it doesn't bother me.'

'And who's this big stupid man?' Tish asked.

We were all silent, wondering what to do, when Tish slumped forward.

'I asked you a question,' she repeated angrily. 'Who are you?' she said to Simon.

'I'm Simon, your mother's friend. And yours too ... well, sort of ...' He faltered and then tried again. 'My name is Simon Butcher.'

'Never heard of you. What am I doing here with a bunch of strangers? Eh, eh? What?' Her voice rose hysterically. Her speech was no longer slurred and I remember thinking that it was odd that she did not smell of alcohol.

'Tishy!' I said sharply. 'Don't you know who you are and where you are – or who we are?'

'My name is Isabella Macdonnell and I live at 9 Rutherford Drive. Why don't you take me there? That's where I live.'

'Who lives at 9 Rutherford Drive?' Maggie whispered. I shook my head.

'Why,' Simon asked, 'do you think you live at 9 Rutherford Drive?'

'You can't fool me, stupid. I know where I live.'

'You don't even know your own name,' Maggie said, wearily.

'Isabella Macdonnell. You can't trick me. I keep telling you, lady. Isabella Macdonnell.'

'What school do you go to?' I asked.

'She was at a party run by some of the teachers,' Maggie remarked bitterly. 'I thought it would be all right – a party run by teachers.'

'There are teachers and teachers,' I said, my mind elsewhere.

'My form teacher is Mr Phil Sparling,' Tishy added suddenly.

I laughed – that was so unexpected. She had been in Phil Sparling's class years ago, in Lower Juniors at Breckling Primary. There was a dreadful noise from Tishy and then she turned on me, hissing and snarling and made a leap for my throat, digging her nails in. I nearly fell off the chair with terror and amazement. It took Maggie and Simon together to pull her away from me. I had never seen such hatred. Then she lurched back in her chair and began to talk unintelligibly. Again, she sounded drunk.

'Of course, of course,' I said, soothingly, and decided not to explain why I'd laughed.

'I am Isabella Macdonnell,' she repeated, 'and I live at 9 Rutherford Drive.'

'Whatever you say,' Maggie murmured, exhausted.

'How old are you?'

Tishy jerked angrily. 'I'm eleven years old of course.

That's when you go to comprehensive school, when you're eleven. And who are you?'

'I'm Mrs Macdonnell, Tish, dear – '

'Don't tell lies to me.' She began to scream. 'I hate people telling lies. Tell me the truth. I hate you,' she said between her teeth, looking at me.

I made coffee. Maggie couldn't drink hers, she was trembling so violently, and Tish knocked hers all over the table. Maggie started to cry.

'You stupid little bitch,' Simon shouted, grabbing and shaking Tish. She stood up, shivering all over, and I remembered the night Simon had moved in with them. I looked at Maggie, but she was staring past us all, fixed in her own memories.

'What I want to know is, why are you keeping me here? I want my mother,' Tish said suddenly, and began to sob, shaking all over. 'I want my mother. I'm so afraid, so afraid, so afraid. I'm going to be sick.'

There wasn't a hope of getting her up the stairs to the bathroom in time, so I dashed for a large stew-pot. She heaved and retched into it for a few minutes, but nothing happened.

'Oh, help me,' she cried out, suddenly clutching at my hand. 'I'm so afraid. I'm lonely and cold. I'm afraid of everything,' she moaned. She was dripping with sweat and she looked terrified. I wanted to protect her from this vast unknown affliction which she could not share. She bit herself hard on the arm.

'Dear Tish, don't.'

'Pull yourself together,' Simon said angrily. 'You're just acting the fool.'

Tish took no notice of him but continued shuddering and whimpering. 'Where have you put the bed? I want to lie down.'

'The bed's in the bedroom, Tish. This is the kitchen. If we give you a hand, do you think you could make it to the sofa in the front room?'

Simon frowned. 'Tishy, can't you recognise anything? Which is your left hand?'

She held up both her hands. 'I am Isabella Macdonnell and I live at 9 Rutherford Drive – '

'No, you're not and you don't,' I said. 'You're Tishy Miles and you live at 16 Whirtle Lane. Do you want to lie down or not?'

'Who the hell lives at 9 Rutherford Drive?' Simon asked.

'Who the hell cares?' Maggie retorted, surfacing from the trance.

I had a tickling memory and went and checked it in the phone book. It was, of course, Phil Sparling.

'How odd,' Maggie said.

'But what I want to know,' Tish said, 'is who are you and what is this place and why are you keeping me here, away from my mother? I want my mother.'

'I am your mother,' Mag said.

Tishy put her head on the table and gave little shrieks of merriment. 'You're too beautiful to be anybody's mother. You're just a little girl like me. But tell me the truth – who are you?'

'Tish – really – seriously – don't you know me?'

There was the sound of a key turning in the front door.

'Oh, thank God, thank God, it's John.' He was the one person who was always sane and steady through any crisis. I was so grateful for him.

'What's wrong?'

I took him into the front room. 'Tish was brought here by the police. They found her lying in the middle of the road, totally drunk, and brought her here. I don't know why here – maybe she pointed the wrong house out to them. She keeps saying she lives at 9 Rutherford Drive. There's something terribly wrong. She tried to strangle me and she doesn't know where she is or who she is or who Maggie is. I wonder if when she fell on the road she hurt her brain in some way. She looks a bit bruised on the face. But she's not acting normally at all, and she seems to be getting worse, not better.'

'Yes,' John agreed quietly. 'It's not like Tish to attack you, Polly. You're the one person she obviously loves. But alcohol takes some people that way and she isn't used to it. Come on, I'll have a look at her. Hello Tish,' he said, coming into the kitchen. 'Do you know who I am?'

'Yes,' she said. 'You're the police. These people have trapped me and brought me to a police cell. But I won't tell you anything. I know that you're the South African police and you're going to interrogate me, but I'll tell you nothing. I'm against apartheid. These people have trapped me. Will you help me escape?'

He was examining her scalp and feeling her pulse and shining a light into her eyes. He managed to get a ther-

157

mometer under her armpit and he listened with his stethoscope at her chest.

'I know this is a police cell,' she said, lowering her voice. 'But I'm not going to tell them anything. No matter how much they torture me. Are you my friend?'

'Of course I'm your friend.'

'Then help me get away.'

'I am your friend and I've told these people they have to be your friends too, because I say so. I think you ought to go to bed now, but we'll watch over you and see that no harm comes to you.' He was speaking gently and rhythmically.

'Oh yes. All right. All right. I trust you. Thank you.'

'Now we're friends and I'll tell these people they must be friends with you too. You must do what they tell you because I won't let them hurt you. You're quite safe here.'

He beckoned us into the sitting-room.

'Drugs,' he said.

'*Drugs*? You're joking.'

'LSD. No doubt about it. The fantasies, the disorientation, the loss of familiar landmarks …'

'Good God,' Maggie said, quietly, and sat down. She had gone quite white.

'I never thought of that,' I said, 'but now that you – '

'Can't be certain without tests, of course, but it's my guess –'

'I'm going to phone the police,' Maggie said, hysterically. 'How dare they – how *dare* they give drugs to Tishy?' She went towards the phone.

'What are you going to say to the police, Mag?' John asked.

158

'I'm going to say my child was at a party and she was drugged.'

'Maggie, who do you suppose will get into trouble by your phone call?'

'Whoever gave her the drugs of course. She's just fifteen.'

'It will be Tishy who gets in trouble. Everyone else will deny all knowledge of such a thing and she'll be seen as the one miscreant. They'll go through her possessions with a microscope and if they find anything, anything at all, she'll be found to be in need of care and protection.'

We went through her things, but found nothing.

'You see,' John explained, 'it's so common at parties these days – everybody knows drugs are circulating, but the police would be delighted at any solid evidence. They wouldn't consider Tishy a victim. To the police she'd be an offender. I know it seems a hard thing to say, but you're not going to catch the supplier that way. So, if you care about Tish, don't call the police.'

Maggie was fuming. 'But – it's – how *dare* they get away with it? I'll bet some joker put it into her drink when she wasn't looking, just for a laugh, to see what would happen.'

'Either that,' Simon said, wearily, 'or she said, yes, she'd like to try it. You've no way of knowing, Maggie. She might even have bought some with her birthday money.'

'So what are we going to say to her? "Happy Birthday, Tish! Enjoy yourself"? I'm going to be sick,' Maggie said, and ran upstairs.

'We'll just have to wait – the drug will probably wear off by itself. We'll wait and see,' John said.

We managed to undress Tish and get her into our spare

159

bed. We didn't think we'd be able to carry her next door and, besides, Maggie said she'd feel happier if John were in the same house. We sat up with her in shifts, an hour at a time, just in case she was sick in the night and choked on her vomit without anyone to help her, but she didn't – she slept very, very deeply until about ten the next morning. Maggie had violent diarrhoea every twenty minutes all night.

Maybe, I thought, maybe she won't recover. Maybe she'll be a vegetable. John had said to me very quietly in the night that sometimes brain damage from lysergic acid was irreversible, that we would have to wait patiently and see what happened.

I was with her when she woke up. She moved her head from side to side and smiled with such sweetness and gentleness that I felt tears gather and roll down my face.

'Who am I?' I said at once.

'You're Mr Sparling,' she answered, 'but you've shaved your beard off.'

Oh God. What if Tish were to be forever an incoherent vegetable, mad as a bloody hatter, because of a little grain of white powder in the bloodstream? I wanted to scream out at such fearful injustice.

She laughed. 'What's wrong, Mrs Macdonnell? What are you asking silly questions for? And what am I doing in your house and why aren't I at home?'

'What's your name and where do you live?'

'I'm Tishy Miles and I live at 16 Whirtle Lane. Why?'

'You didn't know last night. You kept saying you lived at 9 Rutherford Drive.'

'Oh, isn't that funny? That's where Mr Sparling lives.'

160

'Yes, but it wasn't funny.'

'I was awfully drunk, wasn't I? I remember – '

Maggie and Simon came in.

'Tish, how are you?' And then they both said at once, 'Who are you and where do you live?'

'I live at – oh, stop it, this is silly. Mum, I'm sorry about last night. I remember I was very drunk.'

'Who am I?' Maggie begged, and her voice broke and seemed to echo as though she were speaking not only to Tish but to the angels and archangels and, beyond them, to the immensity of God.

'What can you remember?' I asked.

'I remember that I was very drunk. That's all.'

'Do you remember the police bringing you home?'

'Yes, a red-haired policeman, yes?'

'Yes. Found you lying unconscious, dead-drunk, in the middle of Bassett Road.'

'Wow!'

'It isn't funny,' I said furiously.

'But was I really in the middle of Bassett Road, I mean, really?'

'Really,' said Maggie. 'Tish,' she burst out as though she could contain it no longer. 'Tish – did you *take* something?'

'Yes, too much beer, I'm afraid. I'm sorry, Mum.'

'No, I don't mean beer. Dr Macdonnell – he says – he says you'd taken some drugs.'

Her face snapped shut. 'Maybe somebody put them into my drink. I didn't – can't remember – I wouldn't know.'

'Did you take anything on purpose? Who on earth would have put it into your drink? Did anyone buy you a drink?'

161

'Oh Mum, I can't remember, get off my back.' She was returning to normal. Then she sighed. 'Lots of people bought me drinks,' she said, evasively. 'I'd forget it if I were you, Mum.'

But, of course, Maggie couldn't forget it. She met a teacher from Tayfields about a week later on the street.

'I think you ought to be aware that my daughter was seriously ill after the disco on Saturday night,' she said. Another teacher came along and she faced them both. 'We had to have a doctor to see her. He said it was drugs, she'd been taking drugs.'

'Are you sure it was drugs, Mrs Miles?' one of the teachers replied. 'Isabella had been drinking heavily. She was meant only to be having ginger ale, but she tricked us by getting some sixth formers to buy her beer. We didn't discover it until too late. So I imagine her difficulties were due to drink, not drugs.'

She fumed later at all the things she didn't say. Everybody seemed to have heard about it. Parents of other children whom she barely knew came up to Maggie on the street and asked slyly how her daughter was. Perfectly well, thank you, she would reply coldly.

'Why did it have to be Tishy who got drunk and took drugs? Why not some child whose parents don't give a damn? She's my only child. How did I get it wrong? I haven't been a marvellous mother – I know that – but why should I be made to feel guilty? It isn't fair,' she complained to me.

I thought it was eminently fair, but then I had no children

of my own. Ignorance is the best foundation for condemnation.

Tishy returned to school on the Monday following the incident, somewhat subdued. I thought it was behind her, that she was entering a new phase. If I had had one wish at that time, it would have been for the salvation of Tishy Miles.

When Iain got to know of it, he dredged up what he could remember of the Minnesota Care and Counselling Course and when that didn't work, he ranted and kept her in evenings. I knew that wasn't logical and yet I sympathised with his rage at Maggie's bewilderment in the face of adolescent mulishness.

'I want to go to London to live when I'm through with school,' Tishy said. 'I know this girl, Karen, she was at school last year. She's got a flat in London.'

Well, she got the reaction she was hoping for – they exploded. Iain had the usual choice American epithets ready to fling, and he flung them. Maggie, on the other hand, tried love and sweet reason which always culminated in tears. But Tish paid no attention to her mother's distress.

'You're a good actress, Mum,' she would say, acidly.

'I'm at the end of what I can do,' Maggie said, helplessly, to me one afternoon.

'Forget it,' I said. 'You have your own life to lead.'

'That's what I've been saying to you for years,' she agreed, 'but I don't believe it any more.'

'It's too late now, Maggie,' I said.

Chapter 9

We didn't talk about that night again. The next part of the story, which is still about Tish, is almost too painful for me. I'll tell it as quickly as I can. I don't say it was foreordained because I don't believe that nonsense, but in a wider, more general sense, I think that suffering is inevitable.

Tishy took to going to church in her final term at school. I think it was a last resort after her parents failed her or, at any rate, had tried to take certain short-cuts. Tish went through a time of painful self-righteousness, ostentatiously asking a blessing over every morsel of food that passed her lips, spending hours reading the Bible, sending all her pocket money to Oxfam so that she had to have extra when she needed a bus fare. She arranged to get herself baptised and confirmed at the local C of E church, a solemn event which was somewhat lightened by the spectacle of Iain and Maggie vowing to support Tish's regeneration with the Holy Spirit. Tish herself, who had some doubts about their sincerity, explained to the vicar that she was praying for her parents' redemption, a remark which rendered Iain incapable of connected speech. One happy by-product was that she dropped her unsuitable acquaintances (or they dropped her), and all of us – Maggie, Simon, Iain and I – we were all glad. It might have been awkward for them having Tish dash off to church twice every Sunday but, on the whole, they thought it was the beginning of a calmer life. For all that, she was still lonely. In addition, it slowly came out that she was being teased at school because of her new-found religious fervour. But Tish had always been stubborn in her way and she stuck to her views. Who knows what might or might not have been? There's a chill inevitability about one action following upon another.

She managed to get both Maggie and me to go along with her to church one evening, but church – well, it's not my cup of tea. I prefer baking bread for uplift and, anyhow, there's nothing like a thwarted suicide attempt to bring a rush of adrenalin into life if one is really depressed. I prefer to keep a stiff upper lip about ultimate damnation.

The last few months of Tishy's life were hectic. Her social life centred completely around the church and she took to regarding her parents with pious contempt. She was seldom at home at weekends, constantly flurrying off, either to a Prayer Meeting or a Youth Fellowship Club.

Iain and Maggie paid even less attention to Tishy during this time, because Iain had brought home a girl that Maggie didn't get on with, and the four adults were busy working on that problem. They didn't have time for Tishy, that was all. I suppose they noticed her, but they didn't *think* about her.

'I'm not here any more,' Tishy told me one day. 'I'm like a derelict house with nothing inside it. I don't feel anything any more. I thought my soul was saved, but I'm not sure now if I have a soul.'

'A lot of people feel like that,' I answered.

'So what? Perhaps we're nothing but machines. Does it

matter, do you think? I couldn't go on living if I thought I was just a machine.'

'You're not,' I said quickly.

'How can you say that? You don't know. All there is is wanting people to like you, wanting not to die, I'm scared stiff to die. I thought for a while that Jesus would look after me, but I'm still scared.'

'Don't be silly. You have one life and it's up to you how you lead it,' I said briskly.

I remember the day of her death. It was a Sunday and she was going on a picnic that afternoon with some people from the church. We'd played a foursome of tennis over the fence earlier in the day: John and I against Iain and Tishy, and afterwards we'd collapsed on deckchairs, laughing, and Iain and Tishy came over and had iced orange juice with us. I remember her: white shorts and a red and white checked shirt and her hair tied up in two golden bunches. I suppose it wasn't possible to preserve her. She died that afternoon.

There were two passengers in the car when it crashed: Tish and another child from the Youth Fellowship Club. The other girl was not scratched. Why Tish? The other child not a scratch and Tish, thoroughly dead. Not that I would have wished the other child to have been killed of course. It was simply that I loved her. One begins to understand something of the randomness of the death-click, and how one might just as well shrug.

Two policemen came to tell Maggie and Iain; it was a cruel repetition of that night the two policemen brought her to my house drunk and drugged. I wonder what they said to break the news? Mag ran screaming out of the house, and

Iain and Simon ran after her, and pulled her back in. I thought at the time she acted just as though she were on fire and perhaps, in sense, she was. It was Simon who came and told us.

'Could John come?'

He did of course; he always goes at once to anyone who needs him. I sat by myself in the kitchen, uncertain of what I was feeling, simply thinking, So it's happened at last. And that was all. Grief? I couldn't feel grief.

John came back to say that he'd given Maggie something and she was asleep. I had been making scones for tea, so I continued. There seemed no reason not to. I put on a fresh tablecloth, because it was Sunday, and set out the bread and butter and jam and made the tea.

'How was she?'

He shrugged. 'You know.'

'No, John, I don't know. There are a lot of things I don't know. I don't know why we're married and I don't know why I haven't seriously put my mind to killing myself, and I don't know why you don't walk out of the house and let me get on with it. I don't know why I'm here and I don't know what Maggie is feeling.'

He frowned. He is a man who dislikes raised voices. 'Oh, she's sick, and in a state of shock. It's natural.'

'Oh.' I poured him another cup of tea. 'I suppose I'd better go over this evening.'

About an hour later, Iain's lady friend left by taxi, struggling all by herself with her suitcases. I went out and gave her a hand and when I came in I began to laugh hysterically.

'Stop it, Polly.'

'I'll laugh if I want to,' I said. 'I happen to think it's funny – her having to leave like that.'

'No, you don't think it's funny. I don't pretend to understand you, but I know you well enough to know that much. Or do I? Neither of us knows each other at all,' he said, sadly.

I didn't go to see Maggie that evening, or the next day, or the day after. In fact, I didn't go to see her at all. Because my principal thought was still that Tish was lucky to be out of it all, and you can't say that.

Simon was not at the funeral, a fact that I registered but didn't understand. Do you know, I hadn't really thought of what difference Tishy's death would make to that household. If I'd thought about it, I guess I'd have assumed that Simon and Maggie would go away together and marry after a divorce. But all my powers of reasoning came to an end on the afternoon of Tish's death and I stopped speculating.

Iain cornered me around the side of the church after the service. They had decided to bury her where she had been baptised only a few weeks earlier.

'Hello Pol. Why haven't you been to see Maggie?' he asked.

I felt painfully embarrassed.

'How are you?' I asked, ignoring the question.

'No, I asked you something first. Never mind, she's coming now.'

I turned, and there she was, looking peculiar with all her face muscles pulled in strange directions.

'It's time to go,' she said, and took Iain by the arm.

It didn't take long to bury Tish. It was too hot to stand around, anyhow. I kept remembering Maggie and me, both of us crouched over her fire in that cold winter of 1963, both of us frightened of childbirth. What a strange thing to fear, I thought to myself in a daze. It was inexplicable almost sixteen years later. *Are you interested in your soul, your eternal soul? Not today, thank you.* 'I'm sorry, Mag,' I whispered to her, but she pulled away from me. They walked together towards the shining death car, brooding amongst the graves. They will have a lot of sorting out to do now, I thought, and then realised that I was speaking aloud.

'Especially since there's just the two of them, Simple Simon having departed,' John answered.

'*What?* When did that happen?'

'I met him last night just as I was coming in. As far as I could make out from his inarticulate grunts, he was leaving because he couldn't take the emotional temperature.'

'Good God,' I said weakly. It's very difficult to predict human behaviour, don't you think?

'I wonder how Maggie is taking that?' I said a moment later. Was she in such grief that she didn't care, or did his desertion signify for her an immeasurable injury?

Iain came by the next day to say that he and Mag were going away by themselves to the Continent for a few weeks. School was due to start again the following Tuesday, but he'd phoned Derek, and Maggie was going to have compassionate leave for a few weeks. I remembered her last compassionate leave to an aunt in Bermuda. I thought then that Iain reminded me of a cardboard cut-out as he stood in the doorway, refusing to come in. I was certain that a good push would topple him.

Back at school, Jane Harmon said that now that Tishy was

dead there would no one to cramp Maggie's style. I felt no anger at the crudity of her remark because in a sense it was so just. I nodded sadly. How did it happen? How did it happen? Everybody wanted to know the details, but there wasn't anything I could tell them because I had never enquired. Just that she had died instantly.

'Well, that's a relief, that she didn't suffer,' our staffroom Pollyanna said.

I thought about Tish off and on while Maggie was away – Tish lying asleep in the cot by the Chianti lamp, Tish lying unconscious on the Bassett Road, Tish lying dead beside the A34. A sad, strange progression of images. I surfaced to realise I was supposed to be encouraging the children in an RE discussion.

'Methuselah, he lived a long time,' said Sandra of the round face.

'How could he live that long?'

'He probably ate a lot to keep fit.'

I sighed. I could see the point of the discussion fading into the distance, a feeling familiar to all teachers.

'There's a man training to do football who's a hundred and fifty-nine.'

'Maybe there were heart transplants in those days.'

'I'd like to live that long if I could.'

'I wouldn't. You'd have crutches and be all bent over.'

'I believe I asked you what kind of a life you wanted to have, not how long it was going to be,' I interposed wearily. It was Friday afternoon and I was very tired.

'I don't believe he lived that long, anyhow.'

'If it's true, he must have had lots of illnesses.'

'There could have been a mad scientist trying out potions on people.'

I cleared my throat. 'Could we perhaps get back …'

'Why do people say those things when you can't believe them?'

'I don't believe it either, but it must be true because it's in the Bible.'

I reflect that, when I was a child, that would have ended the argument.

'You could test it by digging up his bones.'

'How did the people in the Bible know what a year was? Maybe they measured years differently then?'

'Somebody ought to put it into the years it would be today.'

'They could have said that just to make it more exciting.'

'How old was the rest of Methuselah's family?'

'Maybe they lived longer because they were evolving from animals.' This from John Melville, an earnest child who knew about evolution, sexual reproduction and the solar system. He feared that I might not be cognisant and tried to enlighten me from time to time.

'Someone might have guessed and it got exaggerated.'

I judged the time was right to read them Psalm 90, verse 10.

'Lots of people live to be eighty.'

'Why was Methuselah so old, but in King David's time they only lived to be eighty?'

'More people around and they were all breathing more air.'

'By the time they got to King David, they were making their years longer.'

'There was Noah's Flood and people were different after that.'

'Jesus died at thirty-three.'

'My Mum's thirty-three and she works at Tesco's.'

'My Dad's thirty-six and he's in double glaz – '

I thought it was the moment for some teacher participation so I asked them if they thought living a long time was the most important thing you could wish for. I read them 'All the world's a stage' from *As You Like It* – yes, I did, changing it here and there when they couldn't understand it.

'I'd rather live a shorter time and do all the things I want to do.'

'I want to do both.'

'I'd like to go round the world and see how everybody lives.'

'It's valuable, life, because everything you learn, you get a chance to use it and learn even more.'

'I'd like to help people during my life.'

'If you lived a long time and were lazy and didn't help anyone, you'd think at the end of it that it hadn't been worth living.'

'I want to make something new that wasn't there before.'

Their simple idealism both irritates and shames me.

'You know how Shakespeare said that when you were old it was like being a baby again because you weren't learning. Maybe if you didn't stop learning you wouldn't grow old.'

'I'd like to thank God for having a life at all,' beamed Susan.

Sometimes Susan is sickeningly sanctimonious. Perhaps I could use that in a lesson on alliteration. But then I think, she's right, why am I so reckless with the gift of life?

'It was like when the devil tempted Jesus. Jesus had to decide what were the most important things he wanted to do in his life.'

'When you die, it's a different life after that.'

Is that so, Tishy? *is that so timothy?*

Quite suddenly, it was time for swimming and we had to stop the chat and get changed. Afterwards, Jamie Fletcher paraded about, showing off his party trick. Whenever he comes out of the pool into the chill autumn air, our precocious Jamie finds himself with an erection upon which he is able to hang his vest to the admiration of all the little girls and the envy of the other little boys.

'Oh, put your clothes on, Jamie,' I mutter weakly.

It was home-time then and I watched them leave. I had thirty-eight in my class that year, and I wondered what was the statistical probability that one of them would be dead by the age of twenty-one. Tish had left Breckling (C of E) every day for six years just like that.

After school, I went and did my shopping in the town. There, in the pedestrian precinct, I saw a young child, a girl of about two years old. She was hiding behind a tub of flowers and her father, in order to amuse her, was standing with a look of mock dismay upon his face, wringing his hands and saying, 'Oh, where can she be?' The child could stand it no longer and, with a yelp of joy, she leapt up from behind the flower tub and raced, arms outstretched, to her father who waited for her with his own arms ready to embrace her. I saw her face as she ran and I received such an impression of unsullied joy as I had never seen before. I had a sudden vision of Eden before the advent of sin and death and suffering.

Oh Tishy, I thought, and I began to weep in the middle of the precinct. For what? For the loss of innocence and for the cancellation of warm flesh. I could not bear to think that that little girl laughing in the precinct would, one day, sob herself to sleep in the dark night, her face crumpled in anguish. How long, I wondered, is a baby allowed to keep a soft and open soul, untouched by pain? Someone squeezed my arm.

'Are you all right?'

'Just hay fever,' I said, 'but thank you.'

> The Fates are cruel, cold and clever,
> Tishy Miles will sleep forever.

Chapter 10

Maggie returned to the school in October. How odd were the days without her, slipping by, one by one, crooked, angular, individual. I wonder what I would have said then if I'd been told that within a few months there would be no Maggie, not ever. I suppose there was a notion within me, seeping up from far below, that our remaining time together was to be brief. I didn't analyse it: I assumed it would have something to do with Simon. Two weeks after the start of school, I received a letter from him posted in London.

Dear Polly,

I suppose you must have a very low opinion of me. I have a low opinion of myself, particularly since my main concern is with my own behaviour rather than with the sufferings of others. I had to get away. I couldn't stand things. I know what you think of me and you're right. Please write and tell me how Maggie is. No, don't. Everything we planned is impossible now. I feel my own name is only too appropriate. When it came time to support her and be there for her, I let her down. Simon Peter, you know. As for the Butcher bit … You don't know how sorry I am for the way everything turned out.

It was unsigned, but he had put an address on the back of the envelope, presumably on a last-minute impulse.

Dear Simon,

Maggie is well. She and Iain have gone to the Continent for a short holiday. I don't know what you mean about 'Butcher'. Tishy's death was accidental and totally unconnected with you. It was due to an inexperienced driver pulling out of a side road without looking first. It had nothing to do with you and remorse about Tishy's death is a bizarre and unnecessary refuge to keep you from thinking about what you're going to do next.

Best wishes, Polly.

There was no reply.

Somehow during those weeks that Maggie was away, I acknowledged that I would have to live without her. One day I was listening to a child read, and what he was reading pierced me painfully at the very centre of my substance. It was from the 'Pirate' series by Sheilagh McCullagh, a reading scheme used in our school for Lower Juniors. Here is the passage:

'This is a mirror, Ben,' said the Griffin. 'And with this mirror you can find your way. For if ever you do not know which way to go, look in the mirror and you will see the way you have come. And when you see the way back, then you will know the way on.'

Yes, I thought, that's it, precisely. What I am, I am and I am what I have been. I have no choice. There is my life, like a map, and I have no choice except to continue. I am what I am, and I may as well be glad of what I am. The revelation was so simple and so overwhelming that I sat very still at my desk. We each make our own patterns. I thought of Tishy and all her fear and her awkwardness and how, in a sense, she had been right to distrust the world. She had been right. See the way you have come and then you will know the way on.

'Read it again, please,' I said, and he did.

After break, there was a bustle of practical maths, estimating and measuring distances. It's the sort of teaching I enjoy, talking to the children, relaxed. It was a sunny day and, during the lunch-hour, I took a group out on the field to finish the job. That night I could not sleep, knowing that the other side of that sun was black. Night and day, perpetually, until night finally takes over. More and more in those days, like Tish, I was afraid to sleep. Perhaps, I thought, this is the start of eternity, when those you love have gone. Love, whatever that is. I was illegitimate – I don't know if I told you – and I wore out an awful lot of foster homes early on. Went through them like tubes of toothpaste. It makes an interesting start to a life. All in all, my experiences left me stiff and rigid so I hadn't a great deal of natural sympathy for the soft ones like Mag. When I first realised what a chilly heart I possessed, I was in despair and I looked to Maggie for help and, for a time, she did help me. She warmed me and brought me to life for such a short time. I had hoped that in telling the story I could ease my mind but, oddly enough, the very telling is intensifying the pain and the uncertainty.

The supply teacher who took Maggie's class while she was away was a pleasant woman who, not surprisingly, knew all about mixed fractions. I suppose I'll never meet another teacher who is quite as numerically incompetent as Maggie.

'But you *know* that I don't know my tables,' she would sigh with an air of saintly patience. She would wave the child in my direction. 'Go and ask Mrs Macdonnell what nine sevens are, for heaven's sake. I don't know and I don't want to know.' That was one of the most endearing things about Maggie: her explicit ignorance.

'Mrs Miles can't do one of the questions in my maths book,' Graham said, reproachfully, on another occasion.

'Of course she can, Graham. She just wants you to try to work on it yourself before going to her.' Loyal, that's what I am.

'Can you do this?' Maggie had asked earnestly when I hurried in.

'Of course, and you should too,' I growled at her between my teeth. 'I'll show you how at break-time and then you can show Graham afterwards. Your candour,' I whispered, 'is unprofessional.'

Well, that break-time, I tried to explain lowest common denominators to Maggie. I went back to first principles; I drew pictures; the table was piled high with visual aids; my voice began to rise. Graham came in early from play and looked over my shoulder.

180

He studied my diagrams for a moment and then said, 'I get it now.' He went back outside.

'Good,' said Maggie with relief. 'Since Graham understands, that's all that matters. Quick, let's go and get our coffee.'

She returned to Breckling early in October. It was a clean, fresh day of brilliant intensity, burnished and glowing, as though the Lord, in a fit of domesticity, had taken a polishing rag to the entire universe. She was sitting in her garden alone, when I came home for lunch.

'Beautiful day,' I said, going over to the fence.

'Yes,' she said and got up. 'Come over to my place. I've got lunch ready.'

'Maggie, before I do, I'm sorry … I didn't come over, I didn't write, I didn't do anything to help you.'

'You didn't have to, Polly. It wasn't necessary. We know each other so well.'

I started to cry. 'You're wonderful, Mag, and I feel even worse. Is – where's Iain?'

'At work,' she replied with a slight smile. 'He's finished his compassionate leave. So come over,' she added quickly.

So I did, but spent the whole time, like Cinderella, watching the minute-hand eat up my lunch-hour. Propped up against the kitchen wall, just under her cuckoo clock, was a new painting, evidently still in progress. Later, Iain was to burn that picture, and I think I understand why.

'Mag, why do you paint like this?' I asked in bewilderment.

The sky in the painting rolled out across the canvas, almost into the kitchen, you felt, cold and bleak and menacing. It was a heavy sky, marbled in pink and purple, more like floodwater than air. Overlaid on that sky were twisting silhouettes, dark purple lines turning to black and when you looked more closely you could see they were tiny figures flinging themselves about in a wild dance upon the horizon. In the foreground were snake-trees, bending low over the dancers, picking them up in their claws. In the very middle of the picture was a black horse, terrified, rearing and bolting, trying to escape from the black branches.

'Why?' she asked sharply. 'You'll never understand, Polly, never, never.'

She changed the subject and told me they'd spent most of their time in Holland.

'Flat, boring, just what I needed,' she said. I was silent, waiting for her to go on. 'Did you know,' she said after a long pause, 'we went over on the night ferry?'

'Did you?' I said at last, just to break the silence.

'Hardly room to turn around in the little cabin and I spent the first night by myself tucked up in that tight little cradle rocking back and forth rhythmically all night, feeling the pulse of the North Sea beneath me, and I was reminded of when we came over to England by ship all those years ago, how every night for a week, I'd felt that same strong throbbing through my entire body and that peculiar feeling – that strong, steady rocking, it – took me back to when I was eighteen and coming to England as Iain's bride and it seemed so long ago, so much ... so much ... so much has happened ...' She broke down.

I took her in my arms and began to rock her, strongly, steadily, rhythmically. 'Oh, Maggie!'

182

'Don't say anything.'

'I will say it. Everybody loves you. You've brought so much goodness into my life – oh, hell,' I said. 'I've got to go. It's bloody five to one.'

I ran all the way back and arrived two minutes late.

'Maggie says she'll be in on Monday,' I told Derek after school that day.

'How is she?'

I shrugged. 'Can't really tell.'

'Poor Maggie,' he said, and I felt such warmth towards him for saying it kindly. I've always liked Derek. 'You know I have a soft spot for our Maggie,' he continued with a smile.

I laughed, the first time for weeks. 'Do you know anyone who doesn't?'

'Jane Harmon?' He looked me in the eye. 'Actually, there isn't a man in Breckling who wouldn't jump at the chance to go to bed with Maggie.'

So that was it, was it? Maggie, an object of desire. Maggie, reduced. I laughed again, but this time bitterly.

'Poor Maggie,' I said, 'and yet, granting that extreme beauty is a disability, it's the kind of disability that I think I could endure with fortitude.'

'You're perfectly lovable the way you are,' dear Derek said.

'And you're marvellous, Derek. Every woman needs a headmaster like you. Oh, by the way, didn't you say you were going to move Bernie Chamberlain into another class by half-term?'

'But you're so good with him, Polly, and his parents especially asked that he should stay with you another year.'

'Oh God. Did you know he hid Christine Faldon's knickers after swimming last week? There she was, in floods of tears, standing stark-naked except for a hair ribbon and one sandal. So I had to put on my finest magisterial voice and say, "Now, has anyone seen Christine's underpants? I don't know why *you're* laughing, Stanley Gardiner. *You* wouldn't like to lose *your* knickers, now would you?" When looked at coldly, teaching is a strange way to spend a life. I try to be a good teacher. I've nothing else, you see. It's my life, really.'
no child of my own, you see

He didn't say anything, so I continued. 'If my life has any meaning at all, it must be in terms of the minds I've influenced. I care so much – about – I can't say the word – it – you know – '

'My dear Polly, if you're going to teach the children to be articulate, you'd better make an effort yourself.'

I laughed, this time comfortably, and then shrugged. 'Doesn't matter.'

'No, it doesn't. What matters is good teaching and I'm satisfied with yours. By the way, would you like some free time? I'm up to date with my paper work and I could relieve you from the strain of Bernie for a while. Also, we've got some students coming from the college. Would you like one to help you in the class?'

'Good God, no.'

'Well, I think the answer is Yes. While I'm Head, I put the students where I think they'll fit in best. She's a nice girl.'

'So was my last student – a nice boy.'

'Oho! Simon Butcher. I'd forgotten. Whatever happened to him? Is he still living next door to you?'

184

'No, he left the night before the funeral.'

'The coward. I wouldn't have deserted her.'

'No, Derek, you wouldn't have.'

The following week, I got my college student, a nice girl as Derek had said. She was conscientious and tried hard, but it's a rare student who can do anything of lasting value in their few weeks. She had one of those revolting tutors – a sniffy, thick-lipped, sleepy, hooded-eye type with bad breath and a supercilious sneer. He walks in and in two minutes he sees all he needs to in order to pass judgement on the school, the class and the unfortunate student. You shouldn't do this, you shouldn't do that – aren't you being a teeny weeny bit defensive, he says. He sits and talks with three children for half an hour and produces the remark that those three children are really very intelligent and what a pity that you didn't notice it before. Just look at the work I've managed to get out of them, he says, by simply paying attention. Yes, and what the hell does he think the other thirty-five children would be doing without me and the student keeping them busy while he has his in-depth session with Paul, Alison and Richard? The real give-away, though, is when they keep reminding you of their own happy days in the classroom. There's a positive correlation between incompetence in a tutor and the times he assures you that he spent many a happy year in the classroom and 'knows what it's like'. His memory of his own brilliance as a teacher becomes more and more pronounced as the actual experience recedes. By God, forty-five to a class (hell, make it fifty – your student isn't going to risk contradicting you) and all of them doing individual topic work exactly as was

185

recommended in the latest HMI report published last week. An educational pioneer, that's what he was. They even have the bloody nerve – when you consider their salaries – to tell you that their one regret is that they're no longer able to teach 'as much as I wish'. Mind you, headmasters shed the same kind of crocodile tears when they tell you how much they miss the classroom. To give him his due, Derek never does, but I've heard many a headmaster, tutor and primary adviser say with a catch in his voice how he misses being a class teacher. Simple solution to that problem, mate, I always retort briskly.

In the midst of this, there was another letter from Simon in the post.

Dear Polly,
    This is a very brief note. I'm coming back to Breckling to talk to Maggie and decide things. She's told Iain. I want it finally settled, once and for all. I can't say any more.
                Regards, Simon

It was only to be expected. I showed Maggie the letter.
'I don't really want to talk about it,' she said quietly. 'So much has happened. I wish he weren't coming.'
'I think I understand. It was just – when Simon wrote to me, about you – it seemed natural to show you the letter.'
'Thanks, but I still don't want to talk about it,' she repeated and went into her own classroom, closing the door quietly behind her.
Simon came down from London the following weekend,

but between the first letter and his arrival, a change had come over Iain. He refused to allow him past the door, and the lad stood on the doorstep with his luggage, looking lost and foolish. He left Breckling the same day, and Maggie did not go with him.

'Now, he should have done that a year ago,' John remarked. 'Pity they had to go through all that business before they gained a modicum of common sense. Maybe they can get on with their lives now.'

The days went by, unhappily, because Maggie was losing her glow. I cared about her still, but I cared about her because of the past, not the present or the future. She had so rebelled against her maternal role and yet, without it, she was less of a woman. I could not think of Maggie without vitality. I wondered if she would grow like me, bitter and blanched. I thought, over and over again, that she was turning into the purple Madonna in the painting she'd given to Simon. I could not bear to think of Maggie's goldenness turning to mauve and grey. Maybe, in her paintings, she had prophesied the truth about herself.

I met Iain in Breckling one Saturday morning and he invited me into a little restaurant for a cup of coffee.

'Oh, I expect we'll get a divorce,' he said, nonchalantly. 'She went too far. I know you're getting ready to say "Poor Maggie." Poor Maggie?' he reiterated with an exasperated smile. 'You don't seem to realise that she's going to do the same thing over and over and over to me if I don't stop her. I've had enough. I know everybody laughed at me when I tried to be decent. I did try to be decent, you know. I don't know what the future holds for me, but I do know it certainly doesn't hold Maggie. I've had enough of being a laughing stock. She's undiscriminating – she'll swallow whole the next man who looks at her. She can't do without adoration, you see. But now the decisions are up to me.'

'She may have changed,' I murmured. 'People do change and the whole situation has changed. Besides, Iain, you too ...'

He ignored the allusion. 'Maggie won't change. She's always got what she wanted by being generous with her charms. She couldn't change and – here's the ridiculous part – I don't want her to change.' He flushed, and looked troubled. 'Anyhow, I'd be a fool to expect it.'

He loves her yet, I thought. She draws men to her like iron filings.

'I know she's been thrown off her balance now – by what happened,' he added.

'But she's so quiet these days, Iain. I think there are changes going on inside her. I'm sure she's going to be completely different when she recovers. You can't go through what she's been through – and what you've been through – without it changing you. I do believe in spiritual progress.' We haven't mentioned Tish once by name, I thought.

He put his head back and laughed loudly and unpleasantly. 'Try a bit on yourself before you recommend it to others, Polly.'

I became aware of the sound of a beggar's flute drifting in from far away outside, intensely painful, a sad tune played out remorselessly upon a raw nerve.

'Try a bit of spiritual progress myself, you tell me? You

hear that music?' I asked. 'That's my life, a melody in the minor key. Something in my childhood, something happened that's made it impossible for me to be whole and optimistic. I can't live in the major key. You can, but that door's locked for me. Do you understand?'

'I don't understand you at all. Except you need sex.'

Two balloonfuls of breath which I held. 'Stop.'

'Why? You wanted me once. You'd have fallen on the floor and spread your legs for me. So why don't you now?'

'Yes, you're right,' I said, trying to keep my voice expressionless. 'But that was a long time ago. Water under the bridge and all that.'

'Water. That's Freudian.'

I was trembling. 'Iain, stop it. I'm going to be sick.'

'Sex makes you sick, doesn't it, Pol?'

'No, of course not. What makes you think you're irresistible?'

He laughed again and I left, hardly able to see my way out. By the time I reached home, I had excised the last few minutes of that conversation from my memory.

Chapter 11

The days wore on, shrinking into winter-time. After the Michaelmas half-term, the memories of a year ago rubbed themselves up against us at every turn. There was even a repeat of the music series on the BBC and Derek had suggested that, for economy reasons (since we'd already bought the song pamphlets last year), I should do it again with my new class. I pointed out that I had Bernie Chamberlain and a few other difficult children with me for the second year running, but Derek observed wryly that, with that lot, they'd probably never listened to it the first time and would come to it absolutely fresh.

> One more river,
> One more river to go,
> One more river,
> And that's the River of Jordan!

The melody coiled and twisted its way along the dark labyrinth of memory.

I came in one morning in November to find Maggie there before me, sitting at her desk with something in her hand which she was turning over and over.

'Hello, you're early.'

She got up and walked to the window and I could see that it was Simon's pen-knife that she was holding.

'I didn't go home last night. I slept in the classroom. I overrode the thermostat.'

'*What?*'

'I put the heater on and I had my boots and my coat and the blankets we use every year for the Nativity play. Now that we have the loo built on … I told Iain yesterday morning that I wouldn't be home and he said, "Do what you like." He's not in the least interested in what I do. He doesn't care any more.'

'What do you suppose he thought?'

'I expect – another man. That's what I expect he thought.'

'Don't you think that's rather cruel?'

There was a silence while she struggled for her next words. 'Well, I don't care. There's too much else on my mind. I'm in between two lives. I'm either going to leave Iain, or I can make one last final push to live with him and to try, to really try. But if it doesn't work I must go, one way or the other. I don't know what to do.'

'I think you ought to try,' I said automatically.

She broke into sudden and unexpected sobs. 'I need you, Polly. I need someone strong, someone to tell me what to do. I must do the right thing for myself.'

'You will. You'll land on your feet. Everyone will help you,' I said. More than they have ever helped me, I thought unfairly. Not for the first time, I envied the love she inspired. 'Look,' I said with relief, 'here's Stephen Wood. He's always at school early.' I rushed back into my own room.

'Sorry,' she said briefly when I next saw her. 'Forget what I said. I was a bit over the top.'

I squeezed her arm, which is a cheap and easy emotional gesture. Unfortunately, she came into my classroom after school.

'No, Maggie,' I said at once. 'I can't. It's too much – I have no advice. I have no help.'

'I need whatever you've got, Polly,' she answered. 'I'm nearly at the edge of losing my reason. After all, you were always full of advice when I didn't want it.'

'No, stop. I'm not the person to help you. My own life's too mixed up for me to be of any use to anyone else.'

'No, don't you see, Polly, that's *why* I'm asking you, because you know, you must know what it's like to be dragged down to the very depths. I haven't understood that before. I used to feel sorry for you and feel superior to you, but … you must have known all along what I know now. So tell me what to do.'

'There's nothing to tell,' I said, simply. 'You go on. That's the secret. You keep going. Come on, pull yourself together.'

She began to laugh hysterically. 'You sound like Iain again.'

I hadn't explained it at all well, but there is an enigma at the very heart of making some sense out of the rawness of life. Understanding sometimes just leaps at you from behind a bush, as it were, when you're least expecting it. But before you get ambushed by that understanding you have to go through the whole circular process of despair and trying yet once more and despair and trying once more over and over and over again. And suddenly you wake up one morning and that particular battle is over for the moment. But you can't explain that to anybody who's experiencing despair for the first time. Perhaps I am being unjust to her. One always tends to shrug off the griefs of beautiful people on the grounds that the gods are watching over them. Sometimes I used to look at Maggie and think of Helen of Troy and the magnitude of her remorse.

I remember going home that evening and wishing that I could detach myself for a little while from the necessity to decide and to take responsibility. Sometimes the business of simply existing from one day to the next becomes overwhelming. I felt an almost primitive desire to separate myself from others, to withdraw, to rest awhile, to be not of the world. I needed a temporary exit visa just so that I could stand apart and wait until my breath and my reason returned. I had not attempted to endanger myself for nearly eight years, but I recognised the old compulsion.

Maggie came over at about nine o'clock. By her coming, she stopped me from 'doing anything foolish', as people put it.

'Was Iain glad to see you?' I asked.

'Yes ... Polly ... please ... I have to talk.'

'All right,' I said. 'But expect nothing from me. All my life, I've been a scared rabbit, a coward. I've nothing to give anybody.'

'No, just listen. That'll be good enough. I need someone who knows everything about me. I was a rotten mother. Yes I was, don't interrupt. She had an infection on her belly-button when she was six months old and I didn't do anything about it and she was always crying and I didn't have enough breast milk for her, and I didn't know and I half starved her and the poor little mite, the poor little mite, too innocent, hurt without knowing why she was hurt, just hurt by me, too innocent to know why, just neglected, left in a corner because I had other things to think about. I couldn't be bothered. I ignored her, too busy with night school – she was just a nuisance, and no wonder she was fractious, she just wanted my love and attention. All she needed was me to love her, that was all and I was too busy with other things. When I was in labour, I screamed out that I didn't want a child, I screamed for my mother, but it was too late. I was always shooing her off and wishing she wouldn't bother me. She hated playgroup and cried and was so tired, but I forced her to go because I wanted her off my hands. I wanted free time of my own so I made her go and she hated it. And I forced her. I remember pulling her along and her crying and not wanting to go in and I made her. And she'd be so tired when I picked her up. Why did I make her? Just to give myself some free time. That's all – I put her through that cruelty for selfishness, and the poor child didn't under-stand, didn't understand why she had to leave me, didn't understand anything, was so pitifully bewildered. Just sat in a corner and hoped nobody would notice her, just a failure by the time she was five because nobody did notice, she just sat there, not understanding anything. I had no time for her. I was too busy getting ready to go to college, getting ready for my new life to bother with Tishy. I just hoped she'd get on with it and not make a fuss. She was so open, losing her temper, crying. She was bewildered, not knowing what to do. She didn't know where to turn. She had no defences.

I remember clearly her looking bewildered and sort of saying, "Please don't hurt me." I didn't hit her, nothing like
that, I just didn't love her enough. And all her teachers
threw up their hands. They weren't interested in Tish because she didn't learn and she didn't try and they couldn't
be bothered for the invisible child. She looked so pitiful with
her runny nose and her vacant look, and her desire not be
noticed. My God, that's a desire that's always granted to a
child. We just didn't notice. We were ashamed of her,
ashamed that we had brought up an illiterate child. Embarrassed, that's what we were, that this child who wasn't
doing well at school was ours. And her teachers didn't like
her, especially after she started getting cheeky. Nobody
liked her and she knew it. That was what made her so
obnoxious – she desperately wanted our attention and our
love and she kept acting more and more outrageously, hoping for attention. She had such potential – she could have
gone either way but nobody recognised it, nobody had time
to sit down and listen. She was regarded as stupid and a
problem by everybody. "What shall we do about Tish?" we
all said, instead of giving the right answer, "Love her." We
were all so convinced that she was a problem, that we had
to take her in hand, that we had to make decisions all the
time about her, regardless of what she wanted for herself.
She just got pushed where we wanted her to go without so
much as a by-your-leave. We took her over, treated her as
though she were a doll to be put somewhere and told to be
still and the poor child just accepted it because there was
nothing else she could do, now was there? She was so
unhappy at Tayfields. No friends – she started sweating

under her armpits and nothing seemed to stop it and she didn't do well in her subjects. All the teachers said, "Could do better if she tried" and we shouted at her and that made her more unhappy. She just wasn't happy – she was sweaty and greasy and messy and unhappy, and she just gave up trying. Whatever she did, it ended in despair, and everybody laughed at her when she was awkward and clumsy. Oh, poor child, we didn't know what she was going through. And she had all this trouble at school being bullied, and she used to come home and cry and she told us to go away if we tried to find out why. She suffered terribly because of it – we'll never know how much, but I know she used to come home and cry and cry and cry and she'd never tell me why and I couldn't help her. I'll remember it all the rest of my life, her misery. Never shall I forget. And gradually she grew away from us, wouldn't tell us things. She became more and more solitary, keeping herself unto herself so that we didn't know her any more. She stopped being our child because she stopped talking to us. I guess all her thoughts were going on but she didn't tell us what they were. We were shut out like strangers and all her thoughts went on in her head without us knowing them. She kept herself a secret. She just used to smile shyly and pretend she had no thoughts. They were just thoughts we didn't appreciate and she kept them to herself. I wish I'd loved her more and punished her less. If only I'd known I wouldn't have pushed her so hard, I'd have let her enjoy the day instead of always pushing. We criticised her all the time. Nothing she ever did was right. We were always trying to make her do everything just that much better, never satisfied. We almost

197

never said, "Well done." We always said, "Can't you do it any better than that?" And the kid knew she'd never please us. So she gave up. That was all. What's the point of trying if whatever you do, your parents sneer at it? No wonder she gave up. She could never be as good as the children we admired. She knew she was a failure. So she pretended she didn't care. But she did care, knowing that we were disappointed. She wanted to please us so much, and whatever she did, it wasn't good enough. Poor, poor Tish. We wouldn't take her the way she was. We were always trying to make improvements to her, always slightly ashamed of her, always laughingly apologising. Why didn't we just say "Thank God" and be grateful for her? Why couldn't we see the blessing we had? Oh, Polly, Polly, Polly, I can't bear it. I can't bear it another moment. If only I had another chance, things would be different. I'd take her in my arms and say "I love you, Tish," and ask nothing more of her. If only I had a second chance. I'd give my life for another chance.'

It's too late for that, Maggie, it's too late.

'Stop it. It's pointless. I can't stand it.' Maggie's goldenness was dying; her glow, her flame, her light were going out and soon it would be dark. There was no point now in appealing to rationality. The damned are deaf, and her grief and her useless guilt were too strong for me. *Are you interested in the salvation of your soul, your eternal soul? Not today, thank you.* 'Oh, Maggie,' I said hopelessly. 'It's all too much.'

'Then let's forget it, shall we?' she said abruptly, and was gone.

The following day she came by to say that she was leaving Iain and was going to London to join Simon.

'You have to give a half-term's notice,' I said, mechanically.

She ignored my remark. 'I'm cutting my losses – I'm getting out. I've had enough of Iain. Sixteen years too much.'

She left early on Saturday morning with a large suitcase under one arm and, under the other, the painting of the purple Madonna which Simon had left behind in his precipitate departure.

'Good-bye, Polly,' she said on the kerb as she got into the taxi. 'I'm going to start a new life. Please come and see us when you're in London. I'll keep in touch.'

Simon phoned later in the day to say that Maggie had turned up on his doorstep unexpectedly at about noon. She had come in and they had talked.

'I told her it was all over, Polly, that we couldn't just carry on as though nothing had happened. I told her to go back to Iain. I told her it was over. Too much happened to start again. We couldn't pretend it hadn't happened. I just told her to go back to Iain until she was over the worst of it.'

'She won't go back,' I said in a panic. 'She *can't*. You don't know Maggie's pride.'

'She has to be reasonable,' he said. 'She has nowhere else to go.'

'Reason has never before influenced Maggie's actions,' I answered bitterly. 'She'll find another man, any man. She'll start again with the first man she meets. Whatever else, she'll never return to Iain. She doesn't care what happens to her. Oh, Simon, *something will happen to her*.' I began to cry. 'You bastard!'

199

'I'll see if I can find her,' he said quietly. 'She might have gone to the National Gallery, or Harrods.' He laughed briefly. 'Those are the two likeliest places for Maggie. Maybe I was wrong to send her away so quickly. She – she's too – '

'Simon, how could you? Phone me back if you hear any more.'

I'd hardly rung off when there was a knock at the door.

'I've just had a phone call from my runaway wife,' Iain said. 'She was somewhat incoherent, to put it mildly. She seemed to be saying simultaneously that she wanted to come home and that she never wished to see me again as long as she lived. I know,' he said ruefully, 'that I want her home. But I couldn't bring myself to say it.'

I could understand that. Why indeed should he have felt obliged to beg?

'I know I should have, but too much has happened. Do you think I was wrong?'

'I don't know,' I said. I was surely not the one to offer advice or reproaches. I had already done too much of that.

'I think it's coming to an end,' Iain said. 'I don't think – possibly – not any more – nothing will be solved. Too much happened. Sometimes marriages do finish and this one bloody well has. I only wish that we'd both understood that years ago.'

'Yes,' I said. We sat in silence for a few minutes and then he left.

I spent that evening thinking about my own life, my obsession with Maggie and with Iain too, and I thought of my child, my son, and all those wasted years. The hours ticked by. My husband, for a change, was home and he sat reading medical journals. I started to make a few more haloes for the Nativity play and later, at about eleven, I took out some ironing. Not my idea of a rollicking Saturday night, but there it was. I told myself not to think about Maggie. She has her life, I have mine. Right? Right. You'll probably never see her again, so forget her. Oh God, I thought, she'll get herself into trouble.

'Oh, John,' I said in sudden despair. 'I'm so worried about Mag.'

He took a long time to reply.

'Polly, snap out of it and start to live your own life again. I think it's a blessing for you that she's left. You've been going around in circles with Maggie Miles for the last sixteen years. Remember that you have a life of your own. Indeed, *we* have a life of our own.'

The sane and well-balanced give flawless advice which is of no use to those of us with splintered souls. They hold out genuine food, but we cannot digest it.

'I know,' I said, hopelessly. 'I haven't been able to help myself.'

But already I felt that the day of Maggie Miles was over.

We went to bed then and I had a strange dream about playing tag with her, the two of us leaping over white flowers on the moon. It was such a peculiar dream that I woke up feeling as though I had had a respite from reality, that I had been allowed to enter another world, that I had been given a piece of time which I did not have to account for. I felt stronger.

That morning I reflected on the absurd see-saw of the spirit and how unpredictable were the lifts and the jolts and the drops. It's always a wonder to me how anyone ever seriously sets out to commit suicide (not my kind, the real kind) because, around each new corner, there are not only unexpected events but much more interestingly, totally un-expected moods, often of irrational joy. So it was on that Sunday morning I got up, inexplicably happy and serene.

I made bacon and eggs for breakfast and, just as we were sitting down, the sun shone through the kitchen window, a hazy December sun, and I remembered, a year ago, the sun shining in through the west window at school, shining along a column of golden dust, as Simon and I and the children sang 'One more river'. I felt that a great weight had been lifted from me.

'I'm happy,' I said, and smiled at John, grateful to him for so much of my life that I took for granted.

'That's a change from last night,' he said.

'Yes, funny, isn't it, how a night's sleep makes everything better? The moral of the story is: never commit suicide in the evening. You'll regret it in the morning!'

I laughed, but he did not, and then he said, 'I'd feel happier, though, if my *Observer* had come.'

'Isn't it here yet? It's nearly ten thirty. Come on, now's your chance to avail yourself of all those marvellous inner resources you keep telling me you've got.'

I washed up the dishes and changed the bedsheets and made a lemon mousse for supper. John went into the study, still muttering balefully about the absence of his paper.

'You shouldn't be so dependent upon it,' I said, amused. 'Look, I'll go next door and ask Iain, when he's finished with his, if he could put it through our letter-box.'

Iain was washing his car. 'No,' he said. 'I didn't get an *Observer* either this morning. I was going to walk down later to see if I could buy one at the newsagent's.'

Just then, the paper boy cycled past, and we both hailed him.

'Hey! We didn't get our *Observer* this morning. What's up?'

'No,' he said. 'Nobody in Breckling is getting their *Observer* today. Last night, some dizzy dame on Didcot Station cut her throat from ear to ear and soaked thousands of copies with her blood. People all over the Thames Valley will be missing their *Observer* this morning.'

'Who was she?' I whispered. Iain was completely still. 'Who – was – she?' I repeated.

'Not been identified yet. No luggage. A couple of five pound notes in her pocket but no purse or any identification. She'd been lying there for a bit, sort of gurgling, before the station master noticed her, but she died just as they were lifting her on to the stretcher.' He prepared to cycle off, pleased with himself, but then he remembered another nugget of information. 'But they know her initials – S.B. –' *of course it wasn't why did i oh thank god* 'because those were the initials on the knife she did it with.'

I turned to Iain, but he was already making his way to his front door. I walked back inside. John was just putting on a record, a piano sonata by Schubert, I think it was, and the notes went straight into my heart like nails. John spent a long time with Iain and, when he returned, he was extremely distressed which is unusual for my husband. One sometimes forgets that he has emotions like other men.

203

Later, he drove Iain off to the mortuary to identify her. I stood very still and thought, suicide was always my little game, not yours, Mag.

The following morning there was a letter from Simon.

Dear Polly,

I can't help but be worried about Maggie. You see, I told her quite unequivocally that everything was over – that I wanted to begin a new life away from her and that she ought to do the same – away from me, that is. I'm sure she'll be all right. I think it was really the only sensible thing I could have done. It seemed to me just pointless to get further entangled.

Let me know if you hear from Maggie, won't you?

Affectionately, Simon

Dear Simon,

No, I haven't heard a bloody thing (ha, ha, joke) 'from Maggie', as you put it. You're sure she'll be all right, are you? She's dead. She cut her throat open with the knife you gave her. Made a right mess of Didcot Station, so I understand.

Have you got her painting – the purple Madonna? You'd better keep it. I think if Maggie had the chance to do it again, she'd have done the same thing all over again – I don't mean the Madonna and certainly not the suicide, I mean you. None of us understood her. Please don't write to me again. Just get on with your life.

Polly

P.S. One more river to go. No, I don't mean anything profound by that. It's just that that song keeps going around and around in my brain.

There was a coroner's inquest at which every secret detail of her private life was unwrapped and displayed naked for the newspapers. Poetic justice in a way, I suppose, since she'd buggered their Sunday circulations. I didn't go.

Iain decided to have her buried beside Tish and I got half a day's 'compassionate leave' to attend the funeral. The very words 'compassionate leave' always arouse in me a peculiar mixture of giggles and grief, so different are the various memories associated with that expression. On the day itself we had to struggle against driving sleet to get to the church but, as we sat on the spare, hard seats inside St Stephen's, the sun came out and shone spasmodically through the icy rain.

The glow and the goldenness and the glory of Maggie are no more, I thought. Radiant, loving, selfish, restless Maggie is – not. And no matter what formula the vicar manages to come up with today, it will make no difference.

> Grey, my Friend, is every Theory,
> Green alone Life's Golden Tree.

And it makes not one whit of difference, I went on inwardly, that Goethe put those words into the mouth of the devil. We are today mourning a bloom of Life's Golden Tree which was Maggie Miles. She had been homesick for the prairies and lakes, I thought ruefully, and here we are, burying her by the rivers of Babylon, as it were. But it was too late to change that. A sunbeam rested briefly on the pew in front of us and turned the dust particles into a million sparkling jewels. Earth to earth, ashes to ashes, dust to dust dust dust hath closed Helen's eye and brightness has sure as hell fallen from the air.

On the way home, it was raining heavily and the drops beat against the car window and wriggled diagonally across the glass in hopeless streams like a thousand spermatozoa doomed to destruction. Quite suddenly, in the car, watching the methodical annihilation of the raindrops, I understood why she had wanted to paint. It had been to convince herself that she was real.

Chapter 12

You know why I couldn't leave it at that, don't you? It's because of that profound banality, that life goes on, regardless. So I remained in the queue after Maggie and Tish had dropped out and, since I've got this far, I'll tell you about the continuation of my own life. I nearly said 'postscript' but that would not have been honest for, after Maggie, I found that I began living with a far greater intensity than before.

I remember clearly the first day I experienced a splash of hope. It was an April morning, four months after her death. It was a mild and refreshing day and I walked to school slowly, because I was early and because I wanted to taste the day in small, delicious bites. I strolled along and came up behind a child, one of our less intelligent children who has to struggle with his work. He, too, of course, was early for school and he was celebrating this gift of unbespoken time by rolling joyously in the grass, rolling in the sweet greenness of April, and I thought suddenly that Wordsworth was wrong: that something *can* bring back the hour of splendour in the grass and that joy can blaze in your heart without warning. Because of Maggie and my luck in loving her, I thought. I knew then that I would heal and that the bitter pain would one day be muted, leaving me free to remember the goodness. After the child had run off I stood watching that long, lazy, green grass rippling in the breeze, and I felt such gratitude for the incredible, the staggering beauty of the earth.

I walked into assembly later, still attached to the glory of the morning. I looked at the children, row upon row of white collars, green pullovers and grey skirts and trousers. Then I glanced up at the hymn sheet. Pray God we would not have to be friends of Jesus CLAP CLAP this morning of all mornings.

> Daisies are our silver,
> Buttercups our gold,
> This is all the treasure
> We can have or hold.
>
> Make us bright as silver,
> Make us good as gold,
> Warm as summer roses
> Let our hearts unfold.

Those last two lines brought me close to tears as I thought again of the child laughing in the pedestrian precinct and of poor, young Tishy Miles whose heart was now cold as winter snow. It was obvious to me that I was becoming soppy, so I attempted to harden myself. I gave David Frank-lin the Narrowed-Eye-Look and confiscated a hat pin which was being tested on the child sitting in front of him. It must be my age, but I find myself responding to everything with a heart which is naked, raw and sensitive. Perhaps it was like that in my forgotten adolescence. I am grateful for such a rebirth, no matter how painful.

After assembly and the register, I talk to them a bit about amphibians and how, long ago, some fish developed fins and lungs and how these ones were at an advantage in times of drought because they could wiggle across land to a new watering-place.

The months go by ...

I'm coming near to the end of my story. I've told you the whole thing slowly because I didn't want to miss anything important. There are enough people who could have told you everything in ten minutes flat with their tongues like knives, butchering her memory. Butcher, indeed. He did not reply to my letter. I've tried to peel off her skins, layer by layer, but I suppose no matter how many skins you shed, it's the same snake. Oh dear, I didn't mean it like that. It just came out that way.

It's so wearying sometimes, teaching them their times tables, teaching them spelling rules, doubling consonants after short vowels, teaching them to be polite. You begin to wonder why. This afternoon it is Creative Writing. Fancy that. We're going to try to write a poem about water today. 'Try' – yes, that should satisfy the gods who decide what emerges from the point of one's pen.

Then we talk about water, dark and deep and forever there, from all time, and full of living things – fish and snails and algae. Now I want you to write about some fish in the sea. Oh hell, I think to myself, write what you like – it'll all be the same – it'll all be rubbish.

Let them go – a few will reach something, just a word –

maybe a couple of words in a row – something to show the sea, something to show that their blood is salt. Children, the salt of the earth. And I will watch those children as they grow older, to see if that salt within develops.

Think of the sea and the wriggling life within it, I say; imagine that you slip and slide through the water, that water is your home. 'I was a lake-child,' Maggie used to say. But they can't imagine it, most of them. I have asked too much, as usual. Yet it is not too much for Edith who, earnest and chewing on that pencil, is in the sea now, I can tell. But they are only eight – give them time – make them try – it's worth a struggle. Perhaps this whole lesson has been just for Edith?

> Warm as summer roses
> Let our hearts unfold.

I begin to think about the perfectibility of the human soul and how we all feel, however doubtfully, that we – as we say on the children's reports – 'could do better'. It's a bit like Zeno's dichotomy: however close the soul may be to perfect clarity, it will always have to travel half the distance without limit before it arrives, forever asymptotic to its goal. You must admit it is ludicrous to contemplate our earnest efforts on the treadmill of time. How is it that man ever came to measure himself with the yardstick of eternity? Perhaps because we cannot get rid of our intuition of being at the rim of another world.

I tell David Franklin how to spell 'harpoon' and 'hack'

and 'knife' in quick succession. Not much yearning for the noumenal there.

Possibly the awareness of one's eternal soul falls into a necessary but irrational category. Then where, one asks, does the break occur? To be both ape and angel is a terrible joke. Whatever the theologians say about it, suffering is in the blood and in the flesh. Not much help from Christianity. What exactly, I ask myself, does the Athanasian Creed describe? *So that in all ways, as is aforesaid: both the Trinity is to be worshipped in Unity, and the Unity in Trinity.* I find it difficult to believe that that is a summary of the experiences of the flesh. So is it superimposed, is it a pattern into which the jumble of human experience must be dropped? Perhaps it is suffering which tethers us to eternity. I think again of that ancient and beautiful metaphor of man as a candle: the tallow and the flame. *Are you interested in the salvation of your soul, your eternal soul?* How we laughed.

Break-time suddenly and I am on duty on the Infant playground. Around and around they race in circles, the brightness of youth unleashed. They need music for these wild, circular dances, I think to myself. I walk around very slowly, fishing them out of the hedges and the puddles, very slowly with Anna Fraser hanging on to my knee. I drink the tea that I have been brought and I ask, 'Who would like to take my empty cup back to the staff-room? Anna, you go with James.' My knee is liberated. I amble back and forth on this pleasant, sunny autumn day, this Friday afternoon. I remember other sunny autumn days.

Break is over and the children all called in and I walk back to my own classroom. Some of them have seen me coming and warned the others, so they are all sitting up, smugly straight, when I come in. Oh, how lovely, I say, and they giggle, knowing the noise there was thirty seconds before. Tell-tale Barbara says Peter Nabson was standing on his desk before you came in, Mrs Macdonnell. Thank you, Barbara, how kind of you to tell me.

Oh God, only another hour till the Half-Term, the Glorious Half-Term.

The afternoon is nearly over, let's pack away, clear out your desks. Madeline, will you and Rachel tidy the maths table – you know, number ladders together and counters back in their pots? The stock-cupboard is chaotic, graph paper everywhere. I straighten it and sweep. An older child comes in with a message from the Deputy. Important notices pinned up in the staff-room, thinks I should know as I was on playground duty during break. Thank you, Priscilla. Just what I needed before half-term. Room still a mess. Look, Ben, would you straighten out this computer paper – it's all in a jumble – I'll sort the crayons from the coloured pencils. Lambert and Peter, will you tidy the bookshelves? Friday afternoons are impossible. All right, enough. Before twenty years are over, one of these children will be dead. My heart expands under the pain of too much knowledge, the knowledge of the blackness which will come down upon at least one of you before it is your time. No, that is not right – it will be your time as was planned before time began but, when it happens, it will seem gross and improper. It will seem, when it happens, that the gods have bungled. Now we have twenty minutes left, just enough time for a story ...

They've gone and I fall back in the chair, limp. Screams

from Earl that Lambert has thumped him. Lambert! Lambert! But Lambert is nowhere to be seen. Make a note to speak to him about it after half-term. Poor Earl. Poor Lambert.

There, it's over. Thank God. Oh, hello, Mr Ford. Let me get my record book to write up to date. Glad it's half-term. Tired. No, not going away – see you in a week. Yes. Yes. Goodbye. Good-bye. I remember, and then decide to forget, the important notices pinned on the staff-room wall. When it comes to the Deputy Head's logorrhoea, a little goes a long way.

I go out and start into town to do my weekend shopping, meeting parent after parent as I go. Smile. And there is Mrs Kennedy and the street's teeming with children. No, no plans for going away. Good-bye – enjoy yourself. She's nice – she's got a pleasant child, and she's a pleasant mother who won't blame me if he doesn't turn out to be a top surgeon or a High Court judge. All she wants is for him to understand what he's being taught and to remember it, a requirement which is enough to be getting on with. I wonder what I would have been like as a mother if Timothy had not drawn the short straw?

Cold on his cradle the dewdrops are shining

Why does this bother me now? Lately, I have been wondering what Timothy would think of me today and, because of that, I sent fifty pounds to Help the Aged when I saw their appeal. Wherever he may be, I do not want him to be ashamed of his mother. He is helping me to grow up as I should have helped him.

Every Friday night I stand in the supermarket queue and wonder why I do it. I dash through my day, race, race, race – run home, make supper, wash up the dishes, do my marking and records, drop into bed with exhaustion, spend the weekend cleaning and washing and cooking – Monday morning back to school, days of scurry, scurry, English, maths, art, PE – not a moment to think, never a moment to think. Perhaps that is just as well, given my instinct for murky self-absorption. Yes, thank you, I have a carrier. Thank you. Hello, Mrs Hughes. Hello, Mrs Wood. Now you have to use the underpass to get across the road to my part of Breckling and the tunnel is strewn with filth and has obscene slogans splashed on the walls. It's the spelling mistakes which bother me. After all, looking at the Marion Richardson script used, I realise I probably taught the authors once. It is some comfort to acknowledge that most of those words are not in the Schonell spelling lists. I also reflect that it should be an offence for anyone to use an apostrophe without holding a current apostrophe user's licence. I reach home and go upstairs to the bathroom before starting supper. I look in the mirror, and wonder if I can see my soul reflected: pitted, chipped, marred, like an ancient dart-board.

I nearly forgot to tell you: five weeks after the incident at Didcot, Iain sold the house and went back to the Minnesota prairies as a chemist with an industrial firm. So he's gone and I realise that I never knew him at all, or ever knew what he was thinking.

A few years later, I saw Simon one morning in Oxford, in Turl Street, looking in the window of the Boy Scout shop. He didn't see me at first, so I walked up and stood beside him, silently.

'I'll never hear her voice again, Polly,' he said, and I realised that he must have seen me from the moment I'd turned the corner. 'I loved that voice, that clear, strong, American voice. Oxford's full of Americans now and every time I hear some female with that Mid-West accent, I turn around. I'm hypnotised by those vowels.'

'How are you?' I asked, looking straight ahead into the window.

'Well, I gave up the idea of pushing back the cuticle of human ignorance,' he said drily. 'I've gone into the retail clothing trade, menswear. I found I couldn't stomach interviews with school governors. I began getting jittery and sweaty and making my excuses. I gradually faced up to the fact that I couldn't bear the connotations of a primary school. I saw her in every classroom I walked into. I'm a coward and I couldn't take it. Come and have coffee, Pol. I want to talk to you.'

We found an Indian restaurant and decided to have a meal together.

'Look, Simon, it was bloody bad luck for you. Yes, for you. She's out of it. I know it's tempting to make her out to be perhaps an innocent victim, or else a siren who lured young men to their destruction. She wasn't either, you know. There's a bit in the Bible about the world being a field with both good wheat and weeds and how you can't pull up one without uprooting the other. I think it's the same with

215

people. Good and evil are so mixed up in us all that we can't, in the short life we've got, untangle the mess. That's why it's impossible to summarise a person and say B plus or C minus.'

'Oh, shut up, Polly.' He shook his head miserably. 'I know you're trying to make me feel better, but there's no point, no point whatever in saying, "Cheer up, Simon. It could have happened to anyone. We're all both good and evil." '

'I wouldn't dream of saying that it could have happened to anyone. Adultery doesn't "happen" to people, it isn't a burst appendix.'

'I'm glad you understand that,' he said with a smile. 'I nearly – don't laugh – went into a monastery.'

But I did laugh. Hysterically. 'And why didn't you?'

'I wish you hadn't laughed. That's why I wanted to come back and talk to you again, because I figured you wouldn't laugh. I was going to telephone you this afternoon.'

'I'm sorry. Why didn't you then, I mean the monastery?' The prawn tandoori was extremely good, but I thought it might seem indelicate to comment upon it in the midst of such a fraught conversation.

'After your letter, I went to see my father. I wrote to him first, of course, and told him everything.' He began digging his fork methodically into the tablecloth. I remembered how many years ago I had sat in a restaurant and rhythmically dug a chipped wine glass into my flesh. I glanced at the memory, a white scar on my left hand, just below my wedding ring. 'He said – he said that the same thing had happened to him when he was young. A girl of eighteen had killed herself at university because he'd broken off their

216

engagement. I never knew. So he said, just forget it. You can be either a man or a child, so be a man and forget it. If you stop and brood about it, he said, you'll never grow up. No human being is worth it.'

'That's what my husband tells me. It's good advice, I guess,' I added.

'Oh, stop it,' he cried, angrily. 'How precisely does one go about forgetting it? I look into a Boy Scout shop and what do I see?'

'You see pen-knives,' I answered. Iain was a Boy Scout too, I thought.

'Yes. All right, I didn't go into teaching. But there's more. Oh, hell, you might as well know.'

'What?'

'I'm getting married. Congratulate me. So there, you know.'

'Where,' I asked foolishly, 'did you meet her? I mean, it's very nice of course. I mean, naturally – who is she?'

'She's a divorcee of thirty-five,' he said drily. 'I'd like you to meet her. You'll find her very charming.'

'Try not to be sarcastic, Simon. You must know you took me by surprise.'

'How's John?' he asked quickly.

I always find this a difficult question to answer. 'He is well and I am very fond of him,' I said, with a slight smile.

'I admire your husband, Polly, more than any man I've ever known. How did you meet him?'

'The usual way. Friend of a friend.'

'Like Maggie and me,' he said, with a slight laugh. 'There are far worse ways.'

'Oh Simon,' I said, wearily. 'You understand so little about marriage. The Prayer Book calls it "such an excellent mystery" and, by God, that's right. You can come back and give me your views of matrimony in twenty years' time if you like. Though I don't know the half of it either, since we never had children.'

Cold on his cradle the dewdrops are shining

'Why didn't you?'

'Had a son once. Died. Couldn't after that. But why we didn't adopt – now that's a little deeper. Anyhow, no adoption agency would have considered us with my history, even if we had approached them which we didn't.'

'It's none of my business.'

'No, but – oh dear, don't we know each other well enough by now to talk about awkward things?'

'I don't know,' he replied candidly. 'Who knows what can be safely said to another person?'

'Tell me about your forthcoming marriage. I don't want to be invited, by the way.'

'The wedding will be in October, at half-term, because she's a teacher.'

We were both silent. The season of Michaelmas. I felt inexplicably sad.

'How did you meet her?' I said, brightly, a moment later.

'On one of the interviews for a teaching job, one that I couldn't face up to. She got it. She is very beautiful – black hair if you're interested … and she has a half-grown child.

A girl of nearly fifteen … Tishy's age in case you think I haven't made the connection.'

'Simon, is it a bad joke or what?'

'A merry jest. We did laugh, when I told her the story of my life. She has a sense of humour. Polly, you look shocked.'

'Damn you. I don't like it, I'm uncomfortable.'

'Any laughter we had wasn't very funny. But – OK, that's the sort of woman I fall in love with. I've thought about it, and that's it. At least this time there wasn't a husband around.'

'Much more convenient. So you're going to marry a beautiful, black-haired 35-year-old divorcee with a half-grown child. A girl.'

'What difference does it make? Good Lord, I've thought about it, Polly. I'm not dim, you know.'

'And where are you going to hang the painting of the purple Madonna? In the bedroom? No, let's change the subject. Tell me about the exciting world of men's socks.'

He laughed. 'No, tell me about your work instead.'

'Breckling (C of E) is exactly the same as it ever was and I have forty-two in my class this year.'

'You're joking? You're not joking.'

'And I'm still fighting with Jeremy Richards – you remember, the Deputy Head.'

He smiled. 'It's your nature. You need an adversary.'

Anyhow, we each paid for our own meal and said goodbye. Much later, I remembered that he had not asked about Iain.

The following day was the beginning of a new term, so Derek called an assembly at the end of the afternoon as is his custom. I didn't really listen. I tend to shut off in assembly because drivelling on about morality upsets me. I was roused by the hymn.

God fill my heart with the spirit of seeking,
Visions of wonder let me ever see

Visions of wonder let me ever see. And to think that when school's out we are going to have a staff-meeting on 'Aims and Objectives'. How jolly. It was Jeremy's idea.

'What do you think you should be aiming for as an educationalist?' he asked me.

'To teach reading, writing and arithmetic – as well as something a little more nebulous called General Knowledge,' I replied.

'Yes, but why?' he persisted. His hands and fingers began performing an elegant dance-pantomime. 'We have to foster a partnership in which we promote growth of standards in an environment which is conducive to what is good practice. We must expand opportunities for individual development and sort out our initiatives. In order to do that effectively, we must plan within units to achieve a balanced curriculum so that pupils explore relationships between aims and objectives and make acceptable progress within broad areas of that curriculum.'

'Huh?'

'What I'm saying is, what is the point of education? What are we aiming for?'

'I think that kind of question is arrogant,' I said, hesitantly. 'For every teacher there's a different answer; indeed, for every child there's a different answer.'

'No, we should be aiming to produce a certain kind of child, one equipped to face the modern world. What word can we use to express this? What do we want these children to *be*?'

'Educated?' I suggested, tongue in cheek.

He nodded earnestly. 'Absolutely, Polly, but could we refine that further into learning objectives and identifiable focus points?'

'I couldn't, but I'm sure you can, Jeremy. If I had to express it succinctly, I think the best formulation I've come across – ' Jeremy's manner of speaking is ominously catching ' – is in that hymn: "Visions of wonder let me ever see." And that's my aim. "Visions of wonder let them ever see." '

I myself do not see visions of wonder. My imagination has always been a fusion of aural and sensuous rather than visual. Instead, I feel through my nerve-ends the thrumming of tidal sadness and, in that thrumming, a sense of foreboding. I attempt to analyse the thrumming before accepting it (because that is the kind of person I am) and I find that I can resolve it into notes, that I can give misery a structure. Will it be possible one day to reunite the notes once more into a single harmony of grief which will bring comfort rather than menace? I don't know. I wait in abeyance, in the long pause between notes, ready to join the melody if the time comes.

I wait, but meanwhile life goes on. Jane Harmon and I have become friends. You see, in one of those fearful moments of self-knowledge, I realised how alike we were. It took a while to get over the shock.

'I didn't think you were too fond of me,' she said one day, a bit wryly.

'Things change. I find I'm too fragile to have enemies.' I hesitated. 'Why did you hate her so?'

'Because everybody adored her and gave her what she wanted. She didn't pay her way. I guess it was life I was raging at, the unfairness of it.'

'Yes,' I said. 'I understand. Completely.'

It's four years ago now since Maggie died. What does one say? 'God help us all. There but for the grace …' Sometimes things happen that you don't understand, they rush over your head. You know what I'm talking about, don't you? There is a solution – I believe that profoundly, but I don't know what it is and it makes me feel strange and worried that something that should be at the heart of us all – it should be right at the centre of our being, understanding of the difference between good and evil, but when you look deep, deep – why, there is only darkness where there should be understanding. I know only that I do have a heart that judges and gets hurt from day to day – oh, enough, enough. I refuse to think about it. Don't try to stretch your little mind, Polly Macdonnell. Apes, angels and men. Life is complicated enough without more introspection. It was that brooding which gradually bled my soul white, leaving behind, like a badger's stripe, a ribbon of bleached and empty years down the middle of my life. Remember: I am Polly Macdonnell, schoolteacher, living in Breckling, Oxfordshire, England. Visions of wonder let me occasionally see.

John and I went to London at the weekend and I remarked, 'It's silly to take the train from Oxford. It would be much more convenient to go from Didcot.'

He looked at me long and steadily. 'Are you sure?'

Yes, I was sure. It was time to join the melody. 'Some good I mean to do despite of mine own nature.'

It wasn't too bad. We were late and had to run for the train so there was no loitering on the platform. On the return journey, I got off the train and tripped right over a pile of *Observers*. Do you know, I haven't read an *Observer* for four years? I keep seeing blood on them. John helped me up and then I sat down again on the stack of papers to steady myself.

'Do you suppose it was over there?' I asked, pointing to a Biblical poster on the wall. I read it aloud. ' "Be not deceived; God is not mocked: for whatsoever a man soweth, that shall he also reap. *Galatians* 6:7." Now that would have appealed to Maggie's sense of humour.'

He sat down beside me, and put his arm around me, something that he never does in public. I looked up at him in surprise and saw him as he was, a Scottish haematologist, fifty-one years old, sandy-haired, watery blue eyes, square-shaped, diffident, slow to speak, intelligent, a strong coarse face with animal desires disappointed. What had I done to him? How could he have known all those years ago when he fell in love with me that I would break him? The sins of the fathers are visited not only upon the children …

'Don't, my dear, don't, don't,' he said, gently.

'I'm so glad you're here,' I said. 'I love you.'

'You can't love anybody.'

'I can try.' There was quietness all around us.

'Yes, you can try, Pol,' he said, and I could hear tears gathering in his throat.